Robert Golan

From Hell to Freedom

Contento de Semrik

Robert Golan

From Hell to Freedom

Senior Editors & Producers: Contento de Semrik

Translation: Tanya Rosenblit
Editor: Gayla Goodman
Design: Liliya Lev Ari
Cover Design: Liliya Lev Ari

ISBN: 978-965-550-299-2

International sole distributor:
Contento de Semrik
22 Isserles st., 67014 Tel-Aviv, Israel
Semrik10@gmail.com
www.Semrik.com

1.

"If you want to live, you must do exactly as I tell you. And now, I order you to tell me everything you know about what is going on in Leningrad!" yelled the oversized Gestapo officer at 17-year-old Olga. Her beautiful face was covered in blood and her long blond hair was dirty and frizzled.

"In this war, we will kill any of you that survived," he continued. Olga looked at him with contempt, noticing a large scar protruding from his face. Without a shred of fear, she raised her head proudly, as if she was annulling his very existence, and pointed her nails towards him.

"Tie her up!" yelled the officer to his soldiers. "She is trying to scratching me, the bitch," he added with a smirk that was the result of his strained nerves. While yelling, he was standing in front of her with his stick and started beating her with all his strength.

"I will not cry!" yelled Olga, who was standing on her feet with great difficulty. Her uniform was covered in blood and she was barefoot as she continued, "I would rather die! I will not give you the satisfaction of making me cry."

"You will talk when I tell you to, you hear? Otherwise you will be dead! Got it? All the captives here at the museum will soon be dead! The German army will punish anyone who is opposed to being freed from communism. We will soon catch the criminal Stalin, and we will eliminate you all together," he added emphatically and then quickly left the room.

This scene took place during the WWII blockade on the city of Leningrad, which today is known as St. Petersburg. Leningrad's largest art museum, the Pushkin Museum of Fine Arts, served as the headquarters for the German army in the blockade that lasted a total of 900 days. The ancient works of art had never looked more sad or disgraced, as if ready to take up the battle against the cruel fascism. The Gestapo soldiers, who secured the perimeter, gave the appearance of a horror show at a communist prison in the Soviet Union. Even there, despite the cruel regime, their harsh oppression and severe actions were not able to completely break the prisoners.

The museum was the home of priceless treasures that had been collected from around the world. Perhaps, out of jealousy, maybe even out of open hatred, the Germans were triumphant in destroying many of the magnificent works of art that had been passed down from generation to generation. Whoever dared to object to the destruction was punished on the spot. Despite all of that, the Germans failed to defeat Russian cultural values.

Showing no mercy, the officer continued to hit Olga until the moment an Obersturmbannfuhrer (a senior ranking officer) appeared. He stood there watching and began yelling out loud at all the captives who were being held in the museum, "Eliminate them! Whoever is not with us shall not live!"

Olga's entire body was covered in blood by that time. Her khaki uniform was torn and she suffered from deep cuts on her chest, but still she didn't stop fighting. At the top of her lungs, she screamed, "Stop it! Stop it! You cruel criminals, you won't be able to kill us all, you cowardly fascists. You want to destroy the entire people, and you think you can, but you won't make it! And you..." she turned towards the officer, "When your people are tried for your actions, it will be too late. You will not be pardoned!"

The Gestapo soldiers found themselves standing in awe of Olga's resilience. After exchanging glances with one another, they stopped everything they were doing and made room for the officer, who was slowly approaching Olga until he finally stood directly in front of her. With a stick in his hand, he started to "caress" her face, taking the stick lower and lower towards her chest, caressing her soft breasts and then he stopped. He took a sample from the blood on her body and with dramatic movements in front of everyone in the room, he smelled the blood and loudly ordered, "This blood doesn't smell good, which means that she needs to be destroyed immediately, understood?"

Hearing what the officer said, Olga was filled with disgust. With what was left of her strength, she faced him, looked him straight in the eyes and spat in his face. "You're a psychopath, you're a coward, you are nothing and you will see that eventually," she told him. "I will be the one who kills you." As she continued to scream and fight for her life, Olga was arrested by the officer's loyal soldiers, who continued to beat her face and all parts of her body.

It wasn't long before Olga lost consciousness and was thrown into the corner saved for the corpses, which was already filled with the bodies of dozens of young men and women. She was thrown next to the body of a blond and handsome young man. The torn uniform on Olga's body exposed her long legs and the beautiful parts of her body. After several minutes of lying there, her hands began moving and without noticing it, they were touching the fingers of the young man beside her, who did not show any signs of life.

The Gestapo soldiers, who faithfully served Hitler and worked towards his goal of reshaping the world under the Nazi image, continued with their cruel labor. Anyone who didn't obey them was viciously beaten to death, and the corner that already held thousands of bodies continued to grow, as more corpses were callously thrown onto the heap.

"Continue! Continue!" ordered the officer. "Anyone who says one word will be beaten to death. His body will be extinguished from this world and thrown onto the pile with the others."

"You don't want to talk either?" the officer asked a man who was standing in front of him. The man was looking at him with his big black eyes, and the officer continued, "I understand you really want to die, right?"

"Yes, I want to die too," said Dima, a brave man who was bleeding to death. With his hands tied as a captive, he advanced towards the officer. The look on his face was serious, without a trace of fear.

"Gladly," the officer replied, but before he could finish his sentence, Dima jumped on him with the speed of light. He slammed him on the head, knocked him down and fiercely kicked another soldier who was next to him. Then Dima ran towards the window and broke the glass with his wide shoulders. By the time the Germans understood what was happening, Dima was already gone—with gunshots being fired at him.

With little strength remaining, Dima escaped. Any effort on the part of the Germans who chased him was useless, as Dima disappeared into thin air. Olga, who was lying exhausted in the dead zone, took advantage of the lack of attention in her direction and continued to touch the fingers of the man lying next to her. It had only been a few minutes, but the man's fingers, which were covered in blood, began to show signs of life, as if taking energy from Olga and passing life from one to another.

The grounds of the Pushkin Museum sounded like one big death cave. German soldiers and vicious dogs chased Dima for many hours. He was using all of his remaining energy to run through a field, in search of a wall that could shield him. Suddenly, he saw four German soldiers out of the corner of his eye. Dima jumped aside and hid between the mountains of snow. He was freezing and afraid to take a breath, lest the soldiers would notice him. Suddenly, a soldier looked in his direction. He only wanted to relieve himself, but unfortunately he chose precisely the spot where Dima was hiding. The soldier stood in front of him without even noticing him, pulled down his pants and sat down. The weapon at his side interfered with the process of elimination, so he took it off and laid it aside. Dima saw what he was doing and without lingering for even a second, he jumped up and grabbed the weapon. The German soldier didn't have time to realize what had happened. While he was still seated in that same position, Dima cocked the weapon towards him. The soldier was scared to the bottom of his soul, and from the intensity of fear, he couldn't even scream. Dima took advantage of the situation, came closer to him, and with the handle of the gun, hit him on the head. With the agility of a tiger, he jumped aside to hide from the other soldiers.

Energized, Dima stood up on his feet. Determined, though trembling, he directed the cocked gun at the three soldiers. Looking them straight in the eyes, he opened fire before they had time to react. In a matter of seconds, Dima had annihilated all three of them.

He was afraid of a German attack when the four bodies were discovered, so he buried them in the snow. "You don't deserve to be buried, not even under Russia's snow," he mumbled to himself.

After a few minutes, a group of soldiers that had heard the gunshots came closer to him. With the help of search dogs, it didn't take them long to find the burial place of the four dead soldiers. One of the officers saw that the dead soldiers' ammunition was missing. "It seems that the escaped captive is the one who took the weapons. Let's go! We have to catch the Russian!" he shouted to the others. "I don't think he managed to get too far. According to the markings on the snow, it is likely he ran north. We are twelve soldiers, so I have no doubt we will find him. The order is—to kill!"

"Heil Hitler!" shouted the soldiers in a sign of identification with the officer's words, and ran north with all their might, in the direction that Dima had gone.

The dogs scouted and tried to locate the escaped fugitive. Dima, who could barely breath, heard them approaching. He had fallen down, but using every ounce of strength, he pulled himself back up. By then it had been four days since he had been given anything to eat or drink. That was the method the Gestapo soldiers used to force them to reveal secrets. All of a sudden, out of the corner of his eye, Dima saw a house on the horizon. He didn't dare to enter it, however, fearing that the Gestapo soldiers would kill its residents as well. "I have to destroy them, I just have to," he murmured to himself. Unfortunately, at that point, his body was starting to betray him. The soldiers continued to close in on him, but he couldn't stand on his feet. The dogs were barking as though they knew that they were getting closer. Just a little bit more and they would catch him. Sensing they were very close to him, Dima moved in place but he was unable to lift his head. With the remainder of his strength, he picked up the gun, gathered all his courage and stood in front of the soldiers. "Come," he shouted. "I am ready! Is it war you want? Then war is what you shall get!"

Dima was a brave man, who refused to give in to a cruel destiny. He clung to the notion that whoever denies the existence of the other one had to lose. Determined to fight to the end, he started shooting in all directions. First he shot the dogs and didn't miss—one bullet for each dog as they fell one after the other. The German soldiers who witnessed the spectacle became afraid. Some of them didn't dare to move, and others started returning fire in his direction. Dima continued, steadily shooting until he was severely injured in his arm. He didn't let the wound stop him, but kept shooting with one hand. When he saw that all ten men were lying on the ground, he got up. He thought he had managed to kill everyone, but then one of the wounded rose from his place, shot at Dima and hit him. Dima was able to shoot back, but they both fell to the ground.

About that time, two German trucks passed by. The soldiers got down to check whether there were any living soldiers among them, but found a field of dead. "They were all killed," said the German officer. Then he went towards Dima and turned over his body. Looking at him, he admitted, "He beat us all."

2.

At the Pushkin Museum, the Gestapo soldiers continued to cruelly question the captives, and when they did not get proper answers, they killed them. Olga kept holding onto the fingers of the soldier who was lying unconscious next to her, as she slowly and miraculously began to sense him responding to her touch. When Olga opened her eyes and met his looking back at her, they both filled up with tears. At that moment, many thoughts were running through their heads; fate, love, soul mate. They felt as though they were surviving for each other, and were being given the gift of life. Olga pulled herself closer to the soldier, and laying in the pile of corpses, in front of the Gestapo murderers, they hugged each other.

"Anyone who remains living will be thrown into the shelter. We will question them again until they will all be dead," came the continued threats from the German officers.

Olga and Carl, the handsome soldier, didn't need words to express what they were feeling. Carl was a 23-year-old university student from Finland. In 1938, he had gone to Leningrad, a city that was known for its beauty, rich culture and centers of entertainment. Carl's goal, like other young Finnish men at the time, was to join the army on ideological grounds. He wanted to contribute his share to the salvation of humanity from Hitler's cruel regime and the fascist rule.

Carl looked at Olga, as if he was expecting to fall captive to her his entire life. From the bottom of his heart, he knew he had to meet her. With unspoken words the two promised each other from that moment on, they would never be apart.

That winter was especially harsh. The temperature in Leningrad dropped to 30 degrees below zero, snow covered the streets and for the first time ever, the Soviet Union deployed its forces against the freezing German army on snowboards. Food was scarce, the fuel was running low and there was no water in the faucets. People were looking for basic means by searching in blown-up and torched houses, risking their lives to find a board or a wooden window from an abandoned house. They were only trying to save themselves from the terrible weather, as if, without warning, the winter was also determined to betray them.

"We have to burn books," said a member of the Communist Party to her husband. "There is no other way. We can't go on like this."

"Quiet!" he snapped at her. "Which books do you want us to burn exactly? Stalin's books or Lenin's books? What is wrong with you? Can you imagine what would happen if someone hears that you are burning Stalin's books, the comrade for whom our soldiers are risking their lives and being thrown underneath tanks? By no means can I burn them. Even if I know we will freeze to death, I can't do it!"

The city streets were filling up with bodies of the victims, with the living walking between them like ghosts, searching for any kind of food and means for heating. Morning, afternoon and evening, women, men and many, many children we seen.

During 25 years of rule in the Soviet Union, Stalin had introduced a regime of terror in the country, from which no citizen had been able to escape. This was even true for the members of the party closest to him, including high-ranking army officers. The fear they had been living under was terrible. Everybody knew he was executing, exiling, arresting, torturing and imprisoning people in labor and concentration camps. The accused had been tortured until they confessed the allegations against them, expressed repentance for their alleged deeds and were then executed.

"Help me, help me! Please!" a woman was shouting and crying out to a group of elderly people that was nearby. "My children are going to freeze to death! I must find a piece of wood. Please help me!"

The old group ignored her, as if she was thin air, and continued with what they were doing. The woman tried to break a piece of wood off a window, to pull off part of the house, but she couldn't do it and kept crying for help. All of a sudden, a soldier in a marine uniform appeared before her. With a combat spirit, he jumped onto the building and broke a piece of wooden frame from the window. In a romantic gesture, as when a lover might pick a flower for his beloved, he presented the piece of wood to the weeping woman. "Thank you, thank you, thank you!" cried the woman as she ran home.

This was the situation in Leningrad, where its citizens were trying to survive and save their family members. In Petergof, there was a different scene unfolding. The Germans took down the extravagant and shining statue of Samson the

Hero in his most impressive battle in history. From the direction of the museum, an old man appeared before them. Turning to the German officer who was ordering the action, he fearlessly raised his voice saying, "You will not be able to do anything to Samson the Hero. This is a historic statue, and if you take it down, you will never be forgiven."

At the sound of his words, one of the accomplices with the Germans pointed at the old man and said, "I know him. This Jew works at the museum."

The German officer raised an eyebrow, and the accomplice added, "His name is Berko. I am from the Ukraine and we worked together. We even got the same salary, but in our country they are killing all the Jews. How is it possible that he is still alive?! And even better off than me? He dresses better, and I am certain he also has a table and chairs in his house. He probably even owns a big heater. I have nothing! For me, Germany is more important than anything, and that is why I am loyally serving the Nazis. I am proud to destroy whoever is alive and living well. Not everyone in the Ukraine agrees with me, but I see that you Germans think the same as I do, and are now even taking down the statue of Samson the Hero. Good for you!"

At that moment, the officer took out a gun, and without thinking twice, shot the old museum worker. He then ordered his soldiers to continue their task of taking down the statue.

The cold temperatures and darkness on the city streets was as menace to the lives of women, men, children and elderly. Dressed in padded jackets full of wool, people were seen walking through the streets with carts in an effort to keep the people dear to them safe. "I have already burned all the books that Lenin wrote to heat the furnace. I have only a few more left," said a lady who was tirelessly collecting corpses from the streets.

"What is wrong with you, madam? Q... quiet, quiet!" her neighbor, who was also collecting the bodies, warned her. "Be careful to not be revealed. These are Lenin's books! You can instantly be sentenced to death for that!"

"I am almost dead as it is. What more do you think they can do to me?" she asked. "They killed my entire family, and I didn't even have the privilege of burying them. The cruel destiny has done its share. I want to die too, but I want so much for someone to bury me."

An alarm sounded in the city that suddenly interrupted the women's conversation, but they both remained where they were. "God, please, drop the bomb on me," the woman wept. Despite being tired of her life, she continued collecting the dead in an attempt to grant them proper burials. The bombs were falling all around, but luckily for the women, none dropped near them.

The streets of Leningrad were dark with smoke. There was an eerie quiet; a mortal silence prevailed. Afterwards, people slowly began to appear on the streets once again, trying to help collect the bodies. Soldiers also arrived at the scene, bent and sad at the sight of the inferno on the streets, but determined to continue their relentless fight against the cruel enemy.

"Doctor, please save me," begged one of the soldiers who was taken to the hospital. "You have to save my life!" he kept crying.

"Don't worry, we will help you all," replied the doctor, even though she knew there were only the two of them facing hundreds of patients.

"Hot water! Quickly! Prepare some alcohol for him," called out the nurse. "Start him on tranquilizers immediately. This wounded man must be operated on right away."

Each minute, dozens of patients were flowing into the hospital. Among them was a severely wounded elderly citizen, who seemed to be making a supreme effort to utter a word to Dr. Vera, "Don't mind me, Doctor. You go ahead and treat the young soldiers. I am sixty years old and won't make it anyway."

Dr. Vera went to him, looked at his shrapnel-filled body, and with great compassion replied, "Don't worry, Victor. We will save you too. I am having you transferred to the operating room immediately."

The Gestapo continued mercilessly murdering its captives at the Pushkin Museum. One of the blood-drenched victims who arrived at the hospital was heard screaming, "I managed to escape from the Pushkin. They are asking questions, trying to get details from us by force, but no one is answering. They are mercilessly torturing the captives, and then they are killing them. Just like that, without thinking twice.

"I saw such a brave girl there, who stood up to the Gestapo soldiers fearlessly! She was a beautiful soldier, who looked to be about 17. You won't believe what they did to her! They cut her breast! Yes, they tortured her so cruelly, but she didn't break! When I ran from there, she was still alive. Her name was Olga," said the wounded soldier before he lost consciousness in the middle of his story.

Hearing the sound of the name Olga, Dr. Vera realized it could be her daughter. Her heart started pounding, and her eyes opened wide. She refused to give in to the soldier's passing-out and started shaking him. She screamed at him and shouted to wake him up, saying "Wake up! Answer me, please. Wake up. What did you say about Olga? Is she still alive? Is she wounded? Wake up, please! I am begging you to wake up. Soldier, I am asking you with all of my heart because she might be my daughter! Is she at the Pushkin? Did you see her?"

There was no response from the soldier, as he remained unconscious.

3.

The Gestapo officer at the Pushkin Museum assumed that Olga and Carl were dying and that he shouldn't waste time on them. Since they were lying in the shelter with the rest of the dead bodies, it would be a waste of his time to continue torturing them.

Slowly, Olga opened her eyes. Carl was looking at her as if she were a miracle sent from heaven. Ignoring the blood, he started kissing her face and caressing her. "My beloved," Carl tried to encourage her, "You brought me back to life with your touch. I feel you are a part of my very body, and I don't ever want to part with you for as long as I live. You are my soul mate, and I want to stay with you my entire life," he added, "When we kill all these cruel fascists, we will marry and move to Finland, which, despite the wars, remains a democracy."

Olga opened her eyes in amazement. "Yes!" Carl continued, "We will live in Finland's capital, Helsinki, which is a beautiful city. You will see. I have a house and family there and we will be safe and happy."

"We have to find out what is going on now," Olga said as she pulled herself away from the romantic moment. She tried to move, but had trouble. "The Germans think we are dead. What will happen to us now?" Olga asked. She managed to pull herself up and make her way to the door, but she found that they had been locked inside.

The hospital was still receiving more and more wounded. The two doctors were completely exhausted, but they did not give up on trying to save lives.

"Vera, do you know this soldier?" asked the doctor while he pointed towards the soldier who told about the incident at the Pushkin. Despite all of Vera's attempts to hold herself together and concentrate on her job, she burst into a terrible cry.

"No...ah... I think so. I think he was speaking to me about my Olga. He said she was being held captive at the Pushkin. I don't know anything more. He didn't manage to say too much before losing consciousness."

"If she is anything like her mother," the doctor said to soothe her, "she will surely survive. We will survive, Vera. We will all survive. Justice always wins. Always!"

"I have to do something, my friend. She is my only child. She is my entire life. What if she is alive and there is no one to save her?" Vera cried, while bandaging the wounds of the soldier in front of her. "Have you any idea what a smart and brave girl Olga is? I am sure she will not give in to the Gestapo so quickly. She will not surrender. I am certain."

Vera didn't get a chance to finish her sentence, because the wounded soldier in front of her woke up. "We have to send an army to the Pushkin," he managed to tell Vera in a weak voice. "If we don't send soldiers to the Pushkin, the Germans will kill everyone there."

"Tell me, soldier," began Vera, taking advantage of his moment of recovery. "The soldier you told me about before, Olga—do you think she is still alive?" She asked hesitantly, fearing that she would cause him to become overexcited in his weak condition.

"I have no doubt that she was alive when I saw her. I was thrown there between the dead bodies, and I saw with my own eyes the moment she woke up and started to move her fingers. Yes, I even saw her pulling the hand of the wounded man lying next to her, who was unconscious."

At that point, Vera was so excited that she was unable to continue with her work, so another doctor replaced her. Vera took some sedatives and bread and quickly left the hospital, trying to get to Olga, her dear daughter. She stormed out into the cold streets, 25 degrees below zero, with her face freezing. She was making her way down the road and trying to pull over trucks to help her until she saw a military vehicle in front of her. A Russian officer dressed in a lieutenant colonel's uniform opened the door and extended his hand to help. "I see you are a military physician," he said politely.

"Yes. Anyway I was until about an hour ago," Vera replied.

"Why? What happened?"

"Olga, my daughter, was taken captive by the Gestapo at the Pushkin, and I am going to release her. I believe she is alive. My Olga is alive, do you hear?" Vera kept weeping.

"Don't worry, doctor," the officer held her hand. "We will get them off our land one by one. We will set our children free as well as all our soldiers. They will pay dearly for this.

"What is your daughter's name, you said? Olga?" he asked.

"Yes, Olga Philipova,"

"Olga!" he cried out while looking at her. "We know of a girl named Olga who has been captured by the Gestapo."

"Do you know my Olga? Do you know where she is?" Vera excitedly asked.

"We are on the verge of an attack. I don't know if the Olga that I know is your daughter, but I guarantee you that we will release all the captives."

While Vera and the officer were talking, Olga was still in the zone of the dead. She was holding Carl's hand and using all of her strength to pull him towards her. "Quickly, Carl. Come! We have to escape. Try to lift yourself up—we have to!" she tried to encourage him.

Carl was unable to stand on his legs. Olga kept trying to carry him, but she could not. "I can't, Olga. I can't. You go on without me. If I survive, I will find you, I promise."

"If we die, we die together, my love," Olga replied, caressing his face.

"You go on, my Olga," Carl said, but was unable to say anything more as his eyes closed.

"You cannot die," Olga whispered. "Get up, Carl. Please get up! We have to go."

With great effort, Carl slowly gathered his strength and got up on his feet. Olga didn't believe her eyes. She started kissing his face, hugging him tightly and leading him out in an attempt to find a place to hide.

"They are so many," Carl said. He became frightened when he saw the dozens of German tanks and APCs.

"It will be difficult for us to escape. I think they are planning some kind of great move, so we have to get out of here quickly."

"Where are the Russians?" asked Carl. "They need to bomb this place with planes."

Olga raised an eyebrow: "Are you not a Russian?"

"No, dear. I'm from Finland. I was sent to study medicine, but I ended up studying engineering, so now I am a construction engineer. I joined the war as a volunteer, because I am against the Gestapo regime. I am completely on the side of the Russians."

All of a sudden, a German vehicle approached them. When it stopped and the door opened, Olga and Carl both missed a heartbeat. "Shall we get in?" Olga asked Carl. "It's either we get into the car now, do our thing and run, or we die and meet in the afterlife."

Carl nodded at her, and they both jumped inside. Olga sat in the back seat, and Carl was near the driver, planning a move. Within several seconds, and a few sharp moves, he grabbed the driver's head, twisted it and threw him aside. Carl took the German's gun, sat at the wheel and felt strong enough to hit him on the head again.

"Carl, quick!" Olga hastened him. "We succeeded so far, but it will be difficult for us to leave the zone. Look, they are everywhere."

"Oh, well," she continued after a slight pause. "It's better to die fighting against them than as their captive. Go, Carl! Go!"

At the military checkpoint, the Germans realized that the soldiers' car had been stolen, and they started shooting at Carl and Olga. Carl was returning fire and managed to kill three soldiers as he broke through the checkpoint. "I have no more bullets!" he yelled and pushed the gas paddle to the maximum speed. "But we made it, Olga, my dear. We made it."

"Look how many motorcycles are behind us," called Olga in alarm. "Go faster!"

"I will kill them myself!" the Gestapo officer screamed when he saw Carl and Olga in the getaway car. "We have to catch those bastards alive, we have to!"

At some point, as a result of the heavy gunshots, the car stopped running. The Germans didn't stop shooting, so Carl and Olga started running and fleeing for their lives towards the Russian headquarters.

"We made it! Welcome, Dr. Vera," the commander said when they arrived at the Russian headquarters at the same time. "You are a brave woman. We could use a doctor here."

"My daughter is brave too," Vera answered, while examining the musculature of his body.

"Is your daughter as pretty as you?" asked the commander with a smile. Vera didn't respond, but allowed herself to ponder the question in her mind. Could she grant herself a moment of pleasure, since she was experienced in military activities and was able to perform her job without any special preparations? Very boldly, she turned to the commander. As an act that was characteristic in those days of war, in which impulses and passions were uncontrollable, Vera clung to his body and started kissing him.

The commander didn't expect such a reaction, but he didn't linger. He held her and led her into the adjacent room. She took off her clothes, and stood naked in front of him. Her exposed body had the shapes and curves of a young woman's body. Her breasts were firm and her eyes were filled with passion. "I am thrilled that a beautiful woman like you desires me," the commander whispered in her ear.

"Let's not talk," Vera put her hand on his mouth. "I want you, Commander Maximov. I just want you." They began making passionate love, which was mixed with agitation, fear and a strong will to survive. With joy.

4.

"We are going to attack the Gestapo in half an hour! Are you ready?" called out Commander Maximov.

"Yes, Captain. We are ready!" replied the anxious soldiers. "From the information we have in our hands, the Germans have four wide tanks, dozens of motorcycles and some airplanes," the commander told them. "We are only about twenty soldiers, with Dr. Vera joining us. I want us to make every effort to free our captives. Many of them may still be alive.

"And by the way," Maximov continued. "Vera's daughter, Olga, is there among the captives. It is safe to assume that she is still alive, so take that into consideration and do everything you can to save her!"

When they arrived on the scene, Dr. Vera, dressed in pure white uniform, decided to go into the Gestapo base herself by crawling through the snow. She wanted to check how well prepared they were militarily; how many soldiers, how many tanks and how many weapons they had. Vera progressed slowly and saw there were at least 40 German soldiers. The place was filled with rooms that had heavy barred windows. All of a sudden, out of the corner of her eye, she saw her Olga! She couldn't believe it! She was seated on the floor, half-naked and every part of her body was covered in blood. Filled with emotion, Vera wanted to go to her, but felt like someone was standing beside her. And indeed, it was a German soldier, who was smiling at her, as if catching her doing something wrong. Before he even had a chance of deciding how he was going to kill her, Vera pulled out a sharp knife, and without a second thought, thrust it into every part of his body.

On the other side, Olga was using all of her resources to pull herself along. She was finally hidden from the eyes of the present company, but despite all her attempts, the Germans spotted her and opened fire.

"I am glad you are with me," Vera said as she came close to the commander. In between the gunfire, she was whispering words of love in his ear.

"You are the hero!" replied Maximov. "Pay attention, the Germans are starting to run away. They are falling and dying one by one. I was waiting for this sight, and it is all thanks to you, my beloved!"

At the sight of the dozens of dead soldiers, the Germans decided to prepare for war with the tanks. "Die! Die!" shouted Vera and kept shooting live ammunition. "The most important thing is that my Olga is alive. Thank God, thank God! My Olga is alive—they have her. I saw her!"

"You saw Olga?" Maximov asked her.

"My Olga, and none other," answered Vera, but felt a little uncomfortable. "I am sorry for not being able to see others too. They saw me and immediately opened fire. I barely managed to escape. Several minutes later, the sounds of airplanes were heard. The Germans started bombing. They were bombing everything, and were slowly entering the city too. What could I have done other then run for my life?"

The lively view of Nevesky Prospekt Street in Saint Petersburg was darkened by the freezing "cave of the dead" in the middle of the historic chaos. "What have we done to you, God?" screamed an old woman in the middle of the street.

"What God?" replied her friend. "I don't know any God. Better give me a gun to fight the Germans. I will kill them, the way they are killing us, and we won't have to walk the streets treading on corpses of innocent people who died from hunger and cold. Only then will we have everything. Only then will we get back to Communism, for Lenin promised us freedom and leadership for the masses. He said we would have bread, sugar, electricity in every house—what more does one need?"

"I think that we would fight even better than the men! I don't have anyone left in my house anymore, I don't have any reason to live since everyone starved to death!" yelled the woman with what little strength she had left.

Identifying with the woman's words, Vera and her beloved commander were standing, not allowing the situation to lower their spirits. They were recovering and preparing for an attack against the Gestapo, for its lengthy and defenseless persecution and for their ways of maintaining control through terror. The commander laid out a plan of action for everyone in the room. The starting time for the plan of action would be decided at a later time.

"I want you to know," he whispered to Vera on the side, "my entire family was killed last year during the bombing, so I don't have anyone left in the world except for you. I am asking you to keep yourself safe, for me."

"We shouldn't talk," Vera replied whispering, "You are the one who has to be careful for me! You have to stay alive with me! You have to, you hear?"

The soldiers were beginning to cross the checkpoint to attack the Germans. Russians were lying under the tanks, standing proudly against the Germans as they relentlessly fought and defended lives with their bodies. The Germans were shooting everywhere, and in some cases even managed to hit. Vera and the commander got away from the soldiers and moved closer to where Olga was.

Marching ahead, the commander shouted, "Olga! Olga Philipova, can you hear me? Olga, where are you?" but no sound was heard. The commander kept yelling, "Olga, Olga, your mother is here with me! Olga Philipova!"

Olga, survived the fire that was directed at her, and was sitting in the corner of the room. She heard Maximov's screams, but was shell-shocked. While looking around her, she tried to whisper, "I am here. I am here."

When the commander came closer, he managed to hear Olga's quiet voice and signaled Vera her location. The two ran towards her. "Olga, my beautiful girl," called Vera in great excitement. Olga couldn't believe she was looking at her mother, and couldn't stop herself from crying. Vera hugged her daughter with all of her strength.

"You are alive! You are alive! My dear daughter, come quickly, quickly, we have to go," her mother encouraged her.

Smiling, the commander left the place and joined his soldiers. Vera and Olga went out after him, running away from the fire. Vera was still hugging Olga with excitement. She couldn't stop kissing her hands and still found it hard to believe. "You are alive, my daughter! We were able to save you. It is all thanks to Commander Maximov. It was him—he is the one who saved us."

"Wait, Mom. Excuse me," Olga said as she pulled herself together. "I can't continue with you just yet. I have to save someone who was with me; someone whom I love very much."

Vera remained silent for a moment, allowing Olga to continue speaking. "He's a Finnish guy from Helsinki," continued Olga. "We tried to escape together, but the Germans caught him. He is still alive, I know that. I have to save him, Mom. Otherwise, I will never forgive myself."

"How did the Finnish get to our army?" asked Vera in amazement. Then she added, "It doesn't matter. I am going with you, my child. We will save him together."

Carl heard that there was a serious attack taking place against the Gestapo, and it gave him strength to continue on his way. While he was still recovering, he saw a German soldier approaching him. Carl didn't linger and attacked him with all his might. After taking away his weapon, he knocked him down to the ground. After no more than several minutes, Olga and her mother saw Carl standing in front of them. Olga jumped up to hug him, exclaiming, "Carl, my love, I thought I would never see you again; I thought we would never meet again!"

Vera looked at the two thrilled, and decided to step back a little, to allow them to have a little privacy in the moments of love. Unfortunately for her, several minutes later, a wounded German soldier looked at her from afar, pointed his weapon at her and took a shot. The bullet hit her in the back, and her smile was extinguished in a second. Vera fell, realizing she had been injured.

"Thank God," Vera managed to say with the remainder of her strength, "God, thank you for making them meet, thank you, thank you, thank you. I am going to die, but thank you for letting them find one another, so I can die peacefully." Vera didn't make it, and within seconds she lost consciousness.

"Mom, Mom! My mommy," Olga's voice sounded, when she realized her mother wasn't near. "Where did you disappear to? Mom, where are you?"

Carl and Olga, happy for finding each other alive and assuming that the danger was already past, started to panic when they failed to see Vera with them. "She couldn't have just suddenly disappeared," said Olga. "She must be around here, she must. Mom! Mommy!" Olga continued to call her, until she found her bleeding and lying in the snow.

"I see her," Olga shouted to Carl and ran towards her. "Mom, Mom! Are you OK? I found her, Carl, did you see? This is Carl, the Finnish man. Mom, please meet Carl. This is the man I love so." Vera woke up, sent one last look and extended her hand towards her. Olga tried to lift her, but realized that her entire back was bleeding.

"Keep my daughter safe," Vera managed to tell Carl.

"Don't leave me, Mom! Mom, please don't leave me," Olga shouted and cried, while Vera was dying.

The battle against the Germans continued, and the Nazis were being killed in masses. Commander Maximov, who remained in the area, noticed that Vera had disappeared. "Where is Vera? Have you seen her? Look for my Vera!" shouted the commander, when all of a sudden he saw Olga and Carl leaning over her body. Maximov approached them and in a trembling voice called, "What has happened to my Vera? Vera, Vera," he kept trying to wake her up. "Vera, my beloved, don't die on me! Please, don't leave me."

"She is dead," whispered Carl with sorrow. "She is dead." Immediately he snapped out of it and said, "There are still Germans in the city and we have to eliminate them."

Maximov felt like he had been destroyed and couldn't stop crying as he hugged Olga. "We loved each other so much; we were about to get married," he cried as he leaned his head over her body. "Well, we can't surrender." He stood up and looked at Carl and Olga, saying, "Look for me after the war. My name is Maximov and I am a lieutenant general. I will look for you too." He turned and ran towards his troops, ordering them to keep shooting. "This is for my Vera," the commander was crying out while shooting. "You will pay for this, you will pay for keeping me away from the love of my life."

In the middle of all the infernal events to remove the German threat and to break down the siege, Olga and Carl managed to take Vera's body for burial, while Commander Maximov and his army of trained soldiers were still at the front. In January 1944, they succeeded, and with the red army forces they broke the German siege around Leningrad. The crossings were opened, which started to bring the city back to life. Trucks of weapons and food began flowing in, and Soviet battle ships, a large part of which had been destroyed, still stood proud and brave against the Nazi ships. Time after time, they fought and didn't allow the Germans to enter the city.

5.

"There are three battle ships waiting in front of us, planning to attack," Morris Ryzhin, the navy officer, yelled to his soldiers. "To the posts, everyone!" he ordered. "We will get ready for a fatal attack, and we will fight to the last bullet. We have to blow up all three ships, so to the posts, everyone! We are all en garde to protect the motherland!"

Morris, a wide-shouldered and strong young man, was considered to be one of the bravest warriors in the navy. He was the son of the wise Moses Ryzhin, the Chief Rabbi in Kutaisi in Georgia. He was the grandson of the governor of the region, who was also an army general, and had been appointed by Tzar Nikolai himself. Morris was known to be a strong, serious, uncompromising man. In the past, he had participated in the liberation of the Baltic States. He took part in the attack on Sevastopol, fought to defend the capital city of Moscow, and received many medals for his bravery.

While Morris's soldiers were still making preparations, the Germans began with the bombings again and hit his men. Morris courageously marched towards them and shot back. He directed missiles straight into one of the ships and hit the Germans, and the soldiers continued to shoot. One ship was hit and was sinking, when all of a sudden, a German soldier jumped into the sea and disappeared.

"He is running away," yelled Morris to his men. "Get him! Don't give up—run as fast as you can. Don't let him get away! Fire, fire!" he commanded. "We will soon catch up to them."

Just when he finished speaking, Morris was hit in his forehead and fell to the ground. In the midst of the panic among the troops, who feared they had lost their commander, the shout of one of the sailors on the ship was heard, "He is alive, Morris is alive! It's only his forehead that is bleeding, but he is alive."

"Keep shooting," whispered Morris in a weak voice. "Finish the ships."

Morris's family lived on the fourth floor in a building on the corner of 24 Tolematsova Street and Noski Prospekt. Morris was a young Jewish boy of 15 with black side curls and a skullcap on his head when his family moved to Leningrad. He was a curious boy who loved walking around with his big brother, Simon, everywhere and documenting the city's rich history. On one of their walks, the two passed near the city church, and at the sound of the choir, Morris could not continue walking. He listened to the prayer in the chant, from which a spectacular voice of a young girl emerged. Morris went inside to see for himself who had that magnificent voice, and he found Maria Dimitrieva, a 14-year-old Christian girl with golden hair and an innocent look on her face.

To the family's dismay, a great love sparked between the two. "You will not have any means to live," said his mother. "We will not give you a thing if you marry her. She is a

Christian! Can you imagine the disgrace? You are a rabbi's son, Morris. Do you understand the meaning of this?"

"I will work hard, Mom," he said with pride. "I don't need anything from you—I love her too much to leave her only because she is a Christian."

After several years, despite the hardships and in spite of his entire family's objections to his relationship with a non-Jewish girl, Morris married Maria. Once married, Maria became the most beloved bride in the family. Morris and Maria were a beautiful couple—he with his sparkling brown eyes in his navy uniform, and she with her golden hair. Everyone on Noski Prospekt, the main boulevard in Leningrad, loved watching them.

Morris decided to join the navy, but he continued to study at the military academy in Leningrad. With time, he achieved higher ranks and spent days and nights in the navy. His family was living in a corner house near the Fontanka River in the center of the city, but he was unable to see them. The cruel reality of life was shared by many of the residents of the city during the war, and many paid the price with their lives.

"Mom, we are hungry," cried Lamara, their eight-year-old daughter. "Jorka is hungry too. He doesn't stop crying, Mom." The cold winter kept anyone who was not at the front closed inside. Without food, drink or heat, they stayed at home under the blankets. Aunt Maro came from Russia, and Morris's mother, as usual, welcomed her with a smile. She invited her to sit on the floor, because they had burnt all their chairs long ago to keep the house warm. Aunt Maro held one of the notes the Germans threw at her. Yes, the

Germans loved throwing notes. That was how they played their games of life and death with the residents.

"Today they aren't throwing bombs. You can go to sleep," Aunt Maro said as she read the note to us. Lamara had also heard the Germans, who called on everyone to go sleep in the shelters. No one really believed them. They enjoyed lying and playing with people's emotions.

Where Morris and his family were living, there were no neighbors. Maria worked at the local bathhouse. During the days of the war, as others hurried to leave the city, she fought in her own way for food and safe sleep for her family. Morris wrote to them whenever he could. He repeatedly asked Maria to not leave Leningrad. "This city will not fall into German hands," he said over and over again. "Under any conditions, do not go anywhere."

Every day, when Maria went to work, she carried two children on her back. With great sorrow, she sometimes feared for their safety and so left them alone while she went to work. In the intense cold, in hunger and fear, the children would stay at home and wait for her to return. Jorka was a little boy, who couldn't even walk yet. Lamara, his older sister, would help her mother as much as she could.

With time, as the pressure of the war was intensifying and Morris would stay at the front, Maria's sister-in-law and her two children, Igor and Slavik, joined Maria and her two children. They were trying to survive all together in one room, with great scarcity. Then Morris's friend's wife and their five-year-old daughter, Ira, also arrived from Russia. Eight people in one room. It was crowded and compact, but warming, and all of a sudden, it wasn't so scary. Yet, the germs were in the air, and epidemics started to spread.

Five-year-old Ira didn't survive and died from scurvy, which was a paralyzing illness at the time. Aunt Maro was unable to overcome tuberculosis, and the difficult atmosphere enveloped everyone, without leaving even an ounce of hope. Lamara and Jorka got shots and vaccines, while Slavik and Igor were really afraid of the shots and refused them under any condition.

Slavik didn't survive either. When he heard the bitter news, Ilyusha, Maria's brother, came and built Slavik a casket. While he was at it, Ilyusha wanted to build caskets for everyone, but his mother wouldn't have it. "You shouldn't make a casket for a living person!" she stated as fact. While the residents of the house were lamenting Slavik's death, his father, a gunman at the front, knew nothing. Nurses came to the house from the hospital, asking to take Igor, who became ill. A short time passed, and they also took Lamara, who came down with diphtheria. Lamara assumed she was going to meet Igor, and asked to take his plastic parrot with her.

"Igor doesn't need a parrot," one of the brothers told her. "He is in a place where he has everything." Lamara was unable to contain herself. The high fever, originating from extreme malnutrition, caused her systems to shut down, one after the other, and she became unconscious. "Her digestive system isn't working," the doctor said, "but we will try to save her anyway. This was a common phenomenon with children, whose immune systems had already lost their ability to fight off the virus. We have to feed her intensively."

"Why are you taking the girl's food?" screamed a woman, who was hospitalized near Lamara's bed. "You bastard, why are you taking her food? What are you even doing here? It doesn't seem like you are even her mother. You don't look anything like her."

Lamara woke up at the sound of the woman's screams, and even though she understood that she was mentally ill, Lamara chose to answer her herself, "I have black eyes, like my father, but it doesn't mean this is not my mother. What do you know, anyway?"

"We have another two hours until they deliver the bread," Lamara told her mother.

"We have to go," she kept urging her.

Before going to war, Uncle Ilyusha left a salami bone, which was his food portion. He said that when he came back at 3 p.m., they would all sit together and eat the salami with him. In the meantime, Lamara prepared the portions of bread her mother baked from potato peels. She would grind them and bake them on the stove.

"If Uncle Ilyusha doesn't get here, we want the salami," cried the children. Lamara knew that on the one hand, she couldn't break the rules herself, but that on the other hand, she took pity on the children. She turned the hands of the clock to 3 o'clock, and when everyone saw that it was supposedly the time, Lamara took the salami out and divided it equally between everyone.

"You shouldn't have done that," her mother was angry and slapped her with all her might. "They will be hungry in the house as well, and what will we do then?" Lamara was sitting in the corner crying, with a bleeding nose.

"It's a shame that a girl should be slapped over a piece of salami," Uncle Ilyusha commented to her mother.

"I am afraid," admitted Lamara, when she was lying helpless in bed. She was silently watching the mice that were making noises around her.

Helpless, Maria went out and started to run around the dark streets of the city, crying for help. "Help my children, please!" she called out as she fell, injuring her head. She continued, "They say that the Germans have increased their attacks on us," shouted Maria. "My children will not survive."

Explosions were heard from every corner, with people running on the streets barefoot, being killed one after the other, like flies. Uncle Ilyusha didn't survive the war, and the situation in the house was getting worse. Mother had nothing to make bread from anymore. There was no way to heat the room and all the relatives were dead. Except for faith, there was nothing that could give anyone even a little bit of hope to strengthen the family. "They say that God pressures, but doesn't strangle. At the end of the day, If we believe, maybe salvation will come," Maria said in a moment of resolve. "We haven't heard from Daddy for such a long time." She took the photo of her Morris, kissed it and passed it to Lamara and little Jorka, to give them a tiny bit of hope. "We mustn't give up, my children. We have to keep searching for food."

"I have an idea!" Lamara yelled. "Why don't we go to the woman we saw in the hospital. She told me that there are a lot of carrots in her shelter and that she was willing to give them to me." At the sound of the offer, Maria got up from her place and asked Aunt Grusha, who was the cleaning lady in the building yard, to watch Jorka for a little while. Then she went out with Lamara. Just before leaving the hospital, the generous woman came to them. From the two bags of carrots she gave them, Maria was sure to make everything she could. The carrots lasted for quite a long time.

"Maria, Lamara, Jorka—my beloved," Morris spoke to himself, lying on the bed inside the ship with a bandaged head. "Don't let anyone hurt you," he kept crying.

"You will be fine," said Slovodskiy, the military doctor who was working there.

There was quiet all around. The German ships had all disappeared into thin air, and Morris, despite his condition, took advantage of the moment to uplift everyone's spirits. He took out his guitar, went over to his proud soldiers and began playing. He sang to his mother, who remained alone, and he sang to his children, Jorka and Lamara. In his own way, he even sent sparks of love to his beloved Maria.

When the war was over, Morris continued with another year of service in Manchuria, which was in dispute at the time as to whether it belonged to Russia or to China. Morris also served in Bandera in the Ukraine, which opposed the Soviet government even after the war. Finally, in 1946, he returned home. Other than helping his sisters who had lost their families, Morris took care of Maria for 22 years, as she had become paralyzed on the left side of her body. Morris loved her very much and took care of her, more than he did of himself. Everyday he bathed her, cooked, cleaned and took care of the needs of the entire family. When he wanted to go out for a walk with her in the fresh air, he would carry her in his arms to take her down four flights of stairs, and then bring her back up.

Every summer, they went to a resort outside the city in a vacation house they had in Pablovsk, which was surrounded by forests. They would stay there and enjoy the peace, the vast terrain and the wide gardens, until the day she died.

Morris mourned Maria's death for many years after she passed away.

At the age of 80, he was recognized as a casualty of war, and was finally given a small two-bedroom apartment. He used the remainder of his energy and his modest income to the benefit of the rest of the family. He continued helping his widowed sisters, who remained on their own.

With time, Morris got to wed both his children and to know four grandchildren. He had very happy moments during his life, but he never forgot the tragic events of Saint Petersburg.

Morris was a hero of war, and at the age of 92, he passed away.

6.

"There is nothing to eat," Olga told Carl while they were heading home. "We can't even get bread."

"Who said there was no bread?" responded Carl, taking his military bag in his hands and pulling out a loaf of dark bread and several cans. "Is this nothing?" he said smiling. "And if you agree to marry me, our house will always be filled with food. I will work hard and do anything for you."

"What?" Olga was mesmerized at the sight of Carl kneeling before her.

"Will you marry me?"

"Yes. I will marry you, my love. I agree to live with you until the end of my life," said Olga, who was unable to control the tears that were flowing freely from her eyes.

"We will do it tomorrow," holding her so tightly that she couldn't breathe. "Right, Olga? We are getting married tomorrow, right?"

"That's right!" replied Olga with excitement. She went into the kitchen cabinet and took out an old bottle of wine she had been saving. "You know, Carl, I have to tell you that from the moment I saw you lying next to me, from the moment, I felt you were giving me life, when your fingers touched mine, from that moment on, I knew I was ready to go with you to the end of the world. I am happy, Carl. I truly love you."

"I never thought that in such sorrow one could be so happy. I love you so much, Olga. I want you to meet my parents. They will immediately see that you are the love of my life." Carl lifted Olga passionately, and they both fell on the ground. Olga was embarrassed to take off her shirt, as she had never done it in front of a man before. She hadn't even kissed anyone until then. Carl began by kissing the back of her neck and caressing her breasts. After Olga got over her shyness, he slowly and passionately placed one hand around her neck, and his other hand on her thigh and took it slowly down towards her vagina. As her excitement grew, Olga slid her hand towards Carl's pants, and felt the erectness of his member on her body. The two started to make love. Time after time after time.

"We will make many babies," Carl said as he held Olga. When they were both tired and still lying in bed, he added, "We will call our daughter Vera, after your mother."

"And what will we wear for the wedding? We don't have any nice clothes," wondered Olga out loud.

She lovingly kissed Carl. "That is not really important, my pretty. What is important is that we survived and are about to be married."

Carl and Olga walked hand in hand towards the registration office in Leningrad. They were on their way to being listed as husband and wife. "Identification cards please," said the secretary. Carl and Olga quickly took out their IDs and proudly presented them to the woman, but after a few seconds she returned them.

"I am sorry," she said. "I can't marry you. Carl is Finnish, and a foreigner cannot marry a Russian citizen in Russia." Carl and Olga's faces showed their shock, which replaced their earlier looks of joy and excitement. They left feeling unsure of themselves, not really knowing where they were headed.

"Don't be sad, my love," Carl hugged Olga, as they crossed the Anichkov Bridge (the Four Horses). "We will get married in Helsinki. We will not have any problems there, because even though the proximity to the Soviet superpower has made the Finnish administration especially careful in matters of foreign policy, it has maintained a democratic constitution during the war, and announced itself to be neutral. And besides, my parents are there too, and they can help us. They can even buy us an apartment."

"Do you even know what is going on there now? I hear that Finland has joined the war unwillingly, and there is great terror there now as well."

"Sure," replied Carl, "but that was in 1939-40, when the Soviet Union was unable to conquer Finland. Hitler allegedly offered to help, but my people, the Fins, are innocent. We believed him and even put up 40 war ships at his disposal! Can you believe that? He tricked us all!"

"Wait," Olga stopped him, "But in 1941, Germany attacked the Soviet Union, didn't it?"

"Yes," Carl continued, "I can even be more specific and tell you that it happened on June 22, 1941. On that same day, the Soviets bombed the Finnish cities, taking many lives and causing immense damage to property."

"I understand," said Olga. "That means that at this point, Finland unwillingly joined the war against the Soviets?"

"Yes, my dear, and when the war was over, Finland was one of the only countries that managed to maintain its independence and to run a democratic administration."

And despite all that, the roads that lead to Helsinki weren't exactly beds of roses. Everything was closed, with quite a few territorial limitations imposed on Finland. Carl refused to give up and continued, filled with energy and motivation. "My father has connections, so let's go to the Finnish embassy. I am sure there will be someone who can help us."

Many places in the city had been destroyed during the war. Quite a few people sacrificed their lives, and all those who were running around in the streets seemed sad and bent over, as if not wanting to look at each other. All they wanted was to stay alive and to be left alone to raise their children in peace. Gone were their ambitions or great aspirations. The private houses, which had been built in organized rows, now seemed like a big Russian village. Many fishermen in the surrounding lakes made fishing gear with their own hands and then sat down with their children to fish and enjoy the tranquility.

A representative of the Finnish embassy, who knew Carl's parents, received Carl and Olga with a smile and immediately arranged a ride to Helsinki for them. The view on the way from Leningrad was magical as everything was green and blossoming. Wide fields, abundant water and lots of flowers. It seemed as though there was no war at all. It was hard to imagine that in this lively place, such cruel events had taken place. Everything seemed to be inviting love, a will to build, to advance, to procreate. In fact, the sin was in not living.

"It's hard to imagine that so many people were killed in such a place," said Carl.

"We managed to survive, but Mom didn't," she replied. "We mustn't forget her, as she sacrificed herself for us and for others. We must try to preserve life. I want us to tell our children who Vera was. They will be proud of her, I am sure."

"Bon voyage!" said one of the soldiers on the border as he waved goodbye to them.

"Carl, I want to ask you a question," began Olga during the ride. "Can we really call our daughter after my mother, Vera?"

"Of course," replied Carl, while he looked at her lovingly and held her. "Do you think we are a couple that is expecting a girl?"

"A girl, a boy," Olga smiled, "The main thing is that we get to a safe place."

"Yes, that's right. I never believed we would get to this moment. And especially here," added Carl. "This is the city I love so much. I want us to stay here and to raise a family with boys and girls till the end of our lives."

"Look, Carl! He caught a fish," Olga pointed towards a fisherman on one of the surrounding lakes. "It seems to be a carp, a big carp."

"My dad loves fishing too," Carl sighed longingly. "We will fish together too," he continued. "I promise you that we are going to be happy, and Vera is going to look at us from the sky and will be just as happy."

"Just so you know, my mom loved life very much. She was a very cultured woman," Olga said. "Once a week, we would visit the museum. We also used to go out to concerts and to operas. She loved classical music very much. It's hard to believe that she is gone; it will never be the same again. It's hard to believe that I will not see my mom anymore. What would I do without you, Carl?" she burst out crying.

While Carl held her lovingly, he tried to console her, "It's a shame she is not with us. I would have liked to get to know her better, but now we have to continue living for her."

The gates in the yard in Carl's house opened, and Carl's parents and his brother ran towards them crying. They were thrilled to see their dear one alive. "Thank God, thank God. God has brought you back to us," his mother was weeping on his shoulder. "And you come with such a beautiful girl. Please come in," she invited Olga. "From now on, this is your house too. From the embassy, we heard everything that has happened and we will do everything to help you feel that we are your family. You will enjoy being here with us, I promise. I will be like a mother to you."

"Thank you, thank you," replied Olga. Even though she felt safe, she couldn't stop her tears.

"Mom, Dad, I want you to know that Olga and I have decided to get married," Carl announced, still excited from being back in his parents' house. "They wouldn't marry us in the Soviet Union, since I am considered a foreigner there. Isn't that funny? They don't care that I fought against Nazi Germany—their laws are really unfair. In any case, it's important for me to tell you that Olga and I want to get married as soon as possible." Olga nodded her head, and even blushed.

"We will prepare the most spectacular wedding that has ever been seen," said Carl's dad. "It's not every day that you marry a son that is back from Gestapo captivity, and with one of the prettiest and most courageous girls in Russia.

"We know you saved our son," he said as he turned to Olga with a blessing. "To me, this is an unimaginable bravery, and we still didn't get to thank you for your courage. Thank you, dear Olga. We are happy that Carl found you and that we are getting you as a daughter. We want to see you here with us for the rest of our lives."

That very day, the family members set the wedding date together. Carl and Olga happily went out to the streets of Helsinki to pick a wedding dress. They were hopping in the streets, hugging and kissing. People were looking at them from every corner, and the joy of life could be seen everywhere.

7.

On November 14, 1945, Olga and Carl were married in front of the country's leadership. Government ministers and their families, women, men and children, raised glasses to the young couple. A lot of champagne was poured at the wedding and everyone had more than their share. With a triumphant smile, they talked about the privilege they shared to be saved from the Gestapo, and to be able to leave Leningrad.

"They are heroes! Heroes! To the wonderful bride and groom," the internal affairs minister offered a toast. "No more siege, no more war," continued the minister, who had had too much to drink, and began unloading everything he was keeping inside. "Here's to freedom! The entire world has seen the true faces of the Nazis, who killed innocent people. They murdered smart Jews, only for being Jews, even though Lenin himself was half-Jewish. He even said at the time that whoever didn't have at least 5% Jewish blood was not presentable. And not just Lenin, but did you know that many of the officers in the Russian army were really Jews? Half a million Jewish soldiers have served in the Soviet Union! Some say that the number was even higher, since many were trying to hide their origin. The entire world knew that, but unfortunately, Stalin didn't. He wanted to use the deadly political game to control us all at any cost."

The internal affairs minister poured himself another glass and continued with renewed intensity, "They are afraid. Yes. The Soviet scientists, the creative generals and even the simple soldiers—they have all become corrupt by fear. Now, the entire elite is in jail, and I would not be lying if I say that it gives me great pleasure. Anyone who thought differently than Stalin and Beria has been killed in cold blood or sent to Siberia, and I am talking about very large numbers of innocent people. The senior judges in Russia were also murdered. Yes. They sent the best of our sons to life imprisonment through false and corrupt trials."

"You are right, and they must pay for it," Carl's father interrupted the minister. "The Russian people suffered feudalism and murderous bureaucracy for many years. People have lived in poverty and with incomprehensible humiliation. The best of our sons were deceived with false promises, and at the end sent to life in prison."

"Yes," continued the minister, "Mothers, children and the elderly all lived in humiliation, and then the Russian people discovered the Soviets were cheating too. While they were talking about freedom of speech, work in the factories and a just division of land and properties, they were really taking advantage of innocent people. I can tell you what happened there. Lenin and his gang had been expecting the Bolsheviks to crumble under the pressure of the working people, the proletariat. The proletariat didn't have any of its own manufacturing means, and then it began operating corrupt courts."

"Can someone give me some more champagne?" the minister looked towards the bartender at the wedding. He was half-drunk, and after finishing another glass, he noticed how attentive everyone was, nodding their heads.

"Lenin even wrote it himself," he continued energetically. "He wrote that someday the truth would be revealed. Then they will put him and the entire Bolshevik leadership on trial for the terrible crimes against humanity that they committed. You understand what it was that he has written about himself?" he said and fell to the ground, completely drunk.

Raising his cup, Carl's brother diverted the guests' attention crying out, "Here is to the couple, Carl and Olga, and to a completely new life!"

Even with the poverty in Leningrad, the wedding of the two war heroes in Helsinki looked like a dream. It was a colorful feast with senior government officials, full of love and joy. It also demonstrated clear proof of the high quality of life in the country at that time, which was known to be one of the richest countries in the world in natural treasures. They were all smiling and happy, although only a short while ago, in Leningrad, it had been completely dark, and many were dying of hunger. It was hard for the people who had been living in poverty and only dreaming about bread, to believe that there would be electricity someday, like Lenin had promised.

The morning after the wedding seemed more promising than ever. The caressing rays of the sun through the window in Carl and Olga's room awakened the loving couple from their sleep. "Your body looks like a painting that no artist would ever be able to paint," said Carl, caressing her hair and enjoying every inch of her body.

Olga, still a bit timid, was trying to cover herself. "You know something Carl," she said covering her head, "when you penetrate my body, I feel great. I just feel myself with you."

The intoxicating smell of flowers drew Olga towards the yard. Carl stood at the window, looking at her, rejoicing to see how she had developed from a young girl into a mature woman. "I want to water the flowers," called Olga. "Bring me some water." Carl smiled, dressed quickly and went in her direction.

They found themselves spending the morning hours as a pair of love birds in the garden, walking and enjoying the chirping and unable to stop showering each other with love. "It's time for lunch, love," Carl offered and led her to the house. His parents and his brother Gustav were sitting in complete silence around the table, with the family servant bringing them hot soup.

"How about we start bringing the business to life again?" Carl's dad broke the silence.

"Before the war, we had a private business manufacturing paper. At that time, we employed nearly one thousand workers," Carl told Olga.

"Now that we are all at home, including Carl, our eldest son," his father continued, "it's time to start over. What do you say?" The quiet turned into a tense silence. Carl and Gustav looked at each other, got up from their seats and raised their hands in joy, exclaiming, "We are ready, Dad. We are ready."

"I am ready too," Olga joined the happiness, without really knowing the details of the deal.

8.

"You have to rest," Carl admonished Olga at the peak of the factory's workday. "You are nine months pregnant, beautiful, and you shouldn't be working so hard." Carl was operating all the paper production machines in the factory, Gustav was organizing the marketing line for sales, Carl's father organized the workers, his mother was taking care of food and drinks and Olga helped out as a secretary.

"It's lunch time," Carl's mom announced.

Sitting in the corner, Olga took her mother's photo out and spoke to her, "My dear mom, it's a shame you are not here with me. I am sure you would have been happy with us, with me, with my husband and with all the family. They are good people, and I feel good with them. I am pregnant now, and if we have a girl, I will call her after you, Mom. I will name her Vera. It's a shame we can't continue visiting your grave to bring you flowers," Olga cried. "You must know that in Russia there are still battles and cruelty on the streets, but don't worry Mom. Time will take care of everything, and we will come; Carl and me and the little one." Olga massaged her belly and continued, "This is your granddaughter, Mom, and soon we will come to you, I am sure." Suddenly, she realized that water was dripping out of her body. Carl's mother was the first to notice.

"Olga is having a baby," she shouted. "Hey, everyone, Olga's labor is beginning!" Carl was very excited and lifted Olga in his arms. Gustav prepared the car, and they all drove happily towards the maternity house.

"Congratulations, Father," Carl came out to his father after the birth. "You have a grandson." The tears wouldn't stop coming out of his father's eyes.

"I have a grandson, a first grandson," he cried and couldn't believe it. Everyone came to hug one another.

"Congratulations, congratulations!" they cried.

"We thought it was going to be a girl," said Carl's mother. "Instead, we have Niko. Nikolai. Now, we need to buy boy's clothes. He is our royal grandson. Nikolai, like Tsar Nikolai," she said and warmly hugged her daughter-in-law.

While Olga stayed home to take care of their son, Carl worked hard to make the family business grow, with no real signs of success. Everyone began to worry, because as the profits were decreasing, the expenses were piling up. "Our factory is losing money," Carl told Gustav. "We are short on money. We are not even covering the expenses—we have to find a way to save the business. Father is not feeling well, and has high blood pressure."

"I am worried about Dad's health too," replied Gustav. "The customers are not in a hurry to pay for the merchandise, including the newspaper owners and others. What do we do?"

They decided to reduce their expenses by laying off all the servants. Father's health had begun to deteriorate, and the doctors weren't optimistic about his chances of recovery. Mother was panicking, but Carl tried to calm her saying, "The only important thing is that Father is well, and we will get over the difficulties in the factory." Everyone in the hospital was praying for Father's recovery. Olga was taking care of the child and also helping around the house with the washing, cleaning and preparing food for everyone. The situation worsened, and at midnight, the doctor gave the worst news of all, "Your father is gone."

This was a tremendous blow to all the family members. They were all depressed, and no one was motivated to work or saw any reason to get up in the morning. The family business continued to go downhill, and without any hope on the horizon.

Olga decided to take matters into her own hands. "Carl, I can work in Father's office."

"It's not as simple as you think," Carl replied blankly.

"I worked with him and learned a lot, so I can at least try. It will be fine, you'll see. I promise."

Carl nodded his head in agreement, as a person who was not expecting great changes, but from that moment on, Olga and baby Niko went to the office. She was doing her best to bring the business back to life by approaching new clients, and insisting on being paid in cash.

When Niko was three years old, the factory began to look up. People were beginning to buy more, and as the profits were increasing, Carl began to see light at the end of the tunnel.

"I am not going to the factory today—I am going to the market," called Olga to Carl's mother. Then she took the basket, hugged and kissed Niko and went on her way.

"Have a good time," Carl's mother wished Olga. "I will take good care of Niko for you. I promise."

Olga began walking peacefully around the market, aware of how life in the city was starting to return to normal. Thinking about her mother Vera, she was choosing what to buy, when all of a sudden, she felt a slight push and a sting of a needle in her shoulder.

"Are you Olga Philipova?" Two strong Russian men in fancy suits and black ties stood in front of her.

"Me? Who are you?" she answered.

"We are KGB and we want to talk to you," one of them told Olga, with the other one blocking her way and injecting a drug into her body. After two minutes, Olga was not understanding what was happening with her. She was being escorted by two security guards, going in their car towards Leningrad, her hometown.

"The injection had a quick effect on her," one told the other. "I wonder why they want her.

Maybe because she is so beautiful, and Beria wants her for himself," he laughed.

"I don't think so. She seems like a good girl. Maybe she is working for the Fins or for the Americans. Who knows? But look at those legs, and what a body," he was impressed. "Let's see where she ends up, maybe in our hands?" he laughed.

"Yes," his friend replied. "The boss always chooses the best ones for himself. We'll see. Maybe he'll throw us a bone." And the conversation between the two continued, while Olga was still asleep and unaware of what was going on.

"Pour water on her," ordered the officer when they arrived at the KGB offices at the center of Leningrad. Olga woke up with a scream, but couldn't lift her head. She mumbled a few words and then fell off the chair. Her dress was open and her entire body was exposed.

"Set her here," instructed another officer to his soldiers, who started splashing cold water on her while making her sit in the interrogation seat. Slowly, Olga opened her eyes and saw two KGB generals in front of her, as well as two deputies.

"Where am I? Who are you? What do you want?" called Olga with a feeling of fright and total uncertainty.

"You have been arrested for treason!" the officer yelled at her. Hazy from the injection, Olga didn't understand what was going on around her. "You are accused of high treason against the Soviet Motherland," continued the officer, "and if you tell us everything about you and your husband's acts of treason, we may be considerate and keep you alive. Maybe we will also let you see your son again. If you won't tell us why you ran away from the Soviet Union and married a foreign citizen, without permission from the authorities, I cannot predict a bright future for you."

Olga was stunned, and couldn't believe what she was hearing. "Excuse me," she tried to pull herself together and understand what was going on. "What espionage are you talking about? We wanted to get married in Leningrad, but they refused to marry us here."

"Yes, yes. Keep making excuses. That's nice, but I suggest you move on to telling us the truth," the officer grinned.

"I really don't know what you are talking about," Olga was in shock. "My husband fought for our country. He was lying with me in captivity after being wounded by the Gestapo, and you are talking to me about espionage and treason?"

The KGB general's rage was increasing, and he banged his fist on the table with all his strength, saying, "Who did you ask before marrying him? He is a foreign citizen, and any foreign citizen is against us. And if he is against us and you have been living with him, he is a spy and you are an accomplice. You have betrayed your people and the Soviet regime. How could you do it? How could you betray those that saved you from the Nazis? How could you have betrayed those that have done so much for you?" he demanded to know.

"I didn't betray anyone," Olga defended herself. "On the contrary, my husband and I survived the Gestapo and continued in the war until its last day. Only after the war was over, we went back home. We went to my husband's parents in Finland, where we were married. We have a three-year-old son, whom you can't take away from me. I didn't do anything bad for this country that I love so much. How dare you kidnap me like this? Do you have no intelligence? I lost my mother in the war, and the only ones I have left are my husband and my son."

"What is your son's name?" asked the officer.

"Nikko," she replied.

"Nikko is a Russian name. I don't think you chose that name by accident," he continued as if he had found a new mystery. "You chose that name after the Tsar, who had been killed with his family. His name was Nikolai, wasn't it?" he shouted. "Yes or no?" Olga was still in shock, not understanding how this was happening to her. "We know everything," continued the officer. "But now you will pay for all your deeds. Your son will grow up without you, and we will do everything we can to locate your husband too."

At the sound of the officer's last words, Olga fainted and fell to the ground. "Pour some water on her so she will understand who is in control now," said the officer, before leaving the room with his friends. Olga, lying on the dirty floor, remained with the soldiers.

She overheard the soldiers, "I will get out of her exactly how and why she betrayed her Motherland."

Olga suddenly jumped up and washed in a bucket of cold water. "I don't believe you are the soldiers of my country. Who are you really? You were supposed to be my friends, the pride of my country. How is that possible? Since I was 17, I fought against Nazi Germany, and you blame me for treason only for marrying a foreigner? And who is that foreigner? Did you check? Did you see that this foreign man, who owed us nothing, was fighting with his own body together with our soldiers?"

The officer, who was still standing near the door, didn't like Olga's words. He came back in, slapped her face and silenced her. When the soldiers saw the officer's actions, they kept beating her, too. First her legs, and then every part of her body. "My Nikko! Carl!" Olga screamed in defense.

"Throw her into the dungeon," the officer cried. "If she doesn't like it the nice way, she will talk in the painful way." The soldiers held her legs and led her to the dungeon, where top murderers had been held.

"The prisoner from Helsinki is tied," the soldier reported on the phone to his commander. "I commit to personally taking care of her," he said and looked at Olga.

"Today!" the General's voice was heard through the speaker. "Today and at any cost. This is an order, do you understand?"

Olga was in four square meters of dirty walls, with nothing but a black and filthy mattress, lying on the floor. Half-naked, Olga opened her eyes, discovered where she was, and crawled to the mattress, crying. With her last bit of strength, she screamed for help, "Carl! Carl! Save me! Nikko, what will become of you with your mother being in this hellish afterworld?" Those were the words that expressed Olga's feelings, as though she had been surrounded by angels of death, searching for her blood.

The dungeon door was opened and another investigator came in. "What do you want from me?" she cried. "You cannot be Russian, you are supposed to protect me, not the opposite. How can this be?"

"Dear Olga," the officer cried. "You have been eating well in Helsinki, while an entire people have been starving to death in Leningrad. We didn't run and we didn't leave Mother Russia, like you dared to do. Where did you get the nerve? You deserve the death penalty for that! Do you understand? I am prepared to kill you myself," the officer yelled as he pulled out his gun and aimed it towards her. "One bullet, and you'll be in the afterlife. Now, get up and speak. Tell us everything, and we'll see what we are going to do with you." The officer's soldiers pulled Olga towards the interrogation room, seated her on a chair and gave her a pen and paper. "Write it all down," the officer demanded, beating her with his stick on her head. Olga kept silent. She didn't know how to respond to what was going on around her.

"I have nothing to write," she said. "My husband and I have been working hard for a living. We have been working in his parent's factory."

"What are you producing there?" asked the officer.

"Paper," Olga replied with fear.

"Paper? Paper? For newspapers?" the officer repeated several times. "And what newspapers use this paper you produce?"

"I don't remember," replied Olga.

"Yes, you do!" the officer raised his voice again and hit her face with force. Olga couldn't stop crying. Her whole body was bleeding, and she didn't quite know what and how to tell them so they would believe her. She didn't understand why she was in a room with soldiers from her Motherland, and why they were treating her the same as the Gestapo officers did when she was being held captive. The KGB officer continued, and with a sharp movement of his stick, he ripped her shirt. Olga tried to stop the tears and cover her breasts, but the officer kept hitting her with all his might. "I assume you have learned a thing or two from the Gestapo," he jokingly remarked. "Did they force you to become a traitor, or did you volunteer to betray your country on your own?"

Olga was begging for her life, and he kept hitting her on every part of her body. He was proud to show his work to his soldiers. He ripped her bra off, and badly beat her breasts and her belly. "This is how I am going to get a rank," he thought to himself, "for this is an order from above. Beria gave the order." Olga was completely bruised, but not uttering a word. When he felt he couldn't break her, the officer stopped and prepared to leave the place in a rage.

"Maybe we will still succeed," his friend called out to him.

"People lay under tanks and blow themselves up for Stalin," he responded, "and I can't break a stupid girl to get a promotion?"

"Why were you planning to produce paper and then publish lies about the KGB?" he shouted at Olga. "What were you thinking of by acting against our Soviet Motherland? Against our dear Comrade Beria? Against the hero and the father of all of us, Stalin? It is only thanks to him that the residents of the city were able to survive in inhumane conditions of extreme hunger, indescribable frost, heavy bombings and lethal epidemics for two and a half years! How could you?!" he continued to beat her again and again.

"I have to succeed," thought the officer to himself. "If I get a promotion, I can be a general and everyone will treat me with care and respect. I will get a brand new office and also free cognac, like what we took from Oberschturman Furer's office after we killed him. The phone rang and interrupted his line of thought. "I am interrogating her, Commander," he told the officer on the other end of the line. "She is very stubborn, and she doesn't want to talk. But..."

"You are fired!" yelled the general, and slammed the phone down.

"Honored General," the officer tried to explain, but the phone had gone dead. "Am I fired?" wondered the officer, not understanding what had happened only moments after seeing a promotion in his mind's eye. "What did I do? Did someone rat on me? Am I being accused without an investigation? For what? What did I do? What did I do? Is this the way to throw away me and my entire service for the Motherland?" He got up and started pacing in the room, back and forth, not understanding what he should do. Despite his bloody hands, he remembered God all of a sudden, and wondered out loud, "Wait, this girl, Olga. What has she done wrong in marrying a Helsinki resident? Nothing! She hasn't done anything wrong. I guess God is paying me back for what I did to her. Yes, I deserve it, because she is not guilty."

"Take her to the interrogation room again," came the voice of another somewhat drunk officer, who was entering the room and giving orders to his men.

"Wait, wait a moment," his friend called out to him. "The interrogation room is occupied. A prisoner died during interrogation there a few minutes ago."

While the soldiers were pulling the captive's body out by his legs, Olga was looking at it all and could no longer contain herself, "Murderers! Criminals!" she shouted. "Bastards! Who are you? Who gave you the right to take people's lives like that? Come and kill me!"

A group of soldiers leapt towards her, beat her badly and put her in the interrogation chamber. Olga kept crying and promising herself, "I will not die. I will not die. I have a little boy waiting for me. My husband will come and take me."

"You bloody criminals! I can't believe that we have spilled so much blood for you, and now you turn into our enemies? Now you are the ones killing us? How can that be? How is it possible that our own soldiers are treating us this way?" she shouted, while still trying to cover her exposed body with her hands.

The officer that entered last was tall, fat and stank of alcohol. He slammed his long arms towards Olga, knocking her to the floor. Pressing her breast with the stick in his hand, he asked with a smile on his face, "Are you saying you want to die? Well, OK. Another one that we will throw to the hungry dogs. Even though you are a bitch too, our dogs are so hungry that they will eat you with great pleasure," he said, while still jabbing his stick into Olga's stomach.

"Let me go! You are no better than the Nazis," Olga dared to shout at him. "You will all pay for this! My people will not be silent, and very quickly you can be sure that you will be removed from office."

The officer continued to poke his stick into all parts of her body, as if ignoring her words. "Tie her arms and her legs!" he ordered his soldiers. "I don't even care if she dies. It will be just one less and we can finish our workday faster."

Olga's condition no longer allowed her to move. She was bleeding all over, and felt her death approaching. "Throw her into the women's chamber. Let's see what the prisoners will do to her there," ordered the officer, and rang his friend, the general. "I have good news for you," he said. "I think your Olga is half-dead already. It seems that the officer that was here before me completely neutralized her. She doesn't understand what is happening around her anymore."

"What?" the general's voice sounded through the earpiece.

"Yes, we threw her to the room with the hard core criminals, to the place we have thrown all the killers and mental patients whose lives no longer matter," the officer responded with pride.

"What exactly do you think you are doing?" yelled the general. "The whole world is looking for this lady, Olga. Beware if I hear that you killed her!"

9.

Olga was thrown into a cell with more than twenty women lying in torn clothes, after being severely tortured. Most of them had been raped by soldiers and were bruised with scratches and cuts on their faces. It was an unbearably horrendous sight, as if hell was on earth. There was not a shred of anything remotely human. "Even in hell they feed you," one of the prisoners told her cellmates, and they all started laughing painfully. "I wonder if the new one is still alive, because it seems like they threw a corpse in here," she added and went towards Olga. She placed her head on her chest and checked her breathing. "She is breathing—she is alive."

"I don't believe it," yelled an older prisoner, and all the girls gathered around and started touching Olga.

"Poor thing, see how she looks. They have no pity, for God's sake," said another prisoner, who slowly tried to take a peek at Olga's vagina.

"Get out of here, you insolent," the older prisoner slapped her face. "Have you no shame? Don't you dare touch her, you hear?"

"What have I done?" the prisoner asked with feigned naivety. "Have you forgotten how you came here? Should I remind you how you were humiliated and almost didn't make it? And what about all our friends here, who didn't make it? Do you remember them?"

Hearing the loud shouting, Olga woke up but felt horrible. Slowly, she opened her eyes. Then she looked around, and even though she understood her condition, she smiled. "I don't believe it, she is smiling! What has she got to be smiling about?" said the prisoner who was slapped, who left the crowd and went to lie down in the corner of the room.

Olga began coming to, and the prisoners helped her stand on her feet. "At least there is water here," she said, "I am so thirsty." With great effort, Olga lifted herself and sipped water from the faucet. "When I was captured by the Gestapo, I didn't even get any water."

"What!" the prisoners were amazed. "Were you in captivity with the Germans?"

"That's right," Olga answered. "I was captured by the Gestapo, while fighting the enemy. They tortured me and assumed I was dead. That's why they threw me among the bodies."

"I'm shocked," said one of the prisoners. "How did you manage to survive that and end up here? What did you do?"

"When the Germans thought I was dead, I met my husband, who was dying next to me in the heap of bodies. Carl, oh, I have missed you so much, my Carl! Carl was my boyfriend. We fought the Gestapo together, and we killed many of them. In fact, we were among those that broke the siege. You wouldn't believe what was going on there! Children were dying by the masses, men, women, elderly— they were all dying from every reason in the world: from hunger, cold, bombings and every sort of cruel torture by the Germans. But they didn't manage to break us." A silence came over the prisoner's cell. All the girls seemed to be eagerly listening to Olga.

"And behold the irony of fate," Olga continued. "After fighting for my country and protecting it, I am sitting here in jail. I am suffering severe torture by our own soldiers, can you believe it?" They all kept silent. No one uttered a word. "I can't imagine what Queen Elisabeth would think, for they say she is the one who constructed this prison we are sitting in," Olga continued talking. "I know the Soviets are taking advantage of this prison more than any other tyrant ever has. They control all those who think differently than they do, or anyone who seems a little more patriotic towards Russia. They accuse everyone of betraying the people, and eventually, they murder them cruelly. Yes, unfortunately, they are no less cruel than the Germans in the Gestapo. And there are many of them. I heard that even members of the Communist Party have been killed here in this jail."

"You heard correctly, Olga," the older prisoner agreed. "So you understand, girls? Do you understand the serious situation that has been created around you is because of the totalitarian regime? They are holding the leadership against the will of the people. Anyone who thinks differently, anyone who, in fact, understands the crimes they are committing, they just kill them. They don't give it a second thought."

"Everything you said is true," the older prisoner agreed, interrupting Olga's speech. "But what does it help us now? We have no hope. We are not even sure we are going to stay alive to see any more of this."

"It's better that we try to fight them," Olga answered, "than letting them kill us like a herd."

"That's right," the girls' voices were heard. "She is right, and we have to do something."

"We are the Russian people. We are no different than the rest of the people," Olga continued. "We have the right to live like everyone and to die of old age, but for that, we must be united and prepared. Everyone here understands that our lives are in danger, right?" she asked the prisoners. They all seemed to nod in acceptance. "Great, that's already a start," she continued. "There is still a chance, at least for some of us, to survive this nightmare and to tell people outside about what is happening here in our own army's prison. I am saying this to you, but even so, I don't believe what I am saying. How can it be that after fighting with all our strength for the liberation of Russia, that we are going through such torture from the hands of our own soldiers?"

"I am a Doctor of Philosophy," the voice of one of the quiet prisoners was heard. She felt confident enough around Olga to let loose of everything she had been keeping inside. "I have never seen one single foreign citizen in my life," she kept saying. "It is clear that I did nothing wrong that could hurt my people. All the accusations against me revolved around lectures I gave my students."

"What were the lectures about?" Olga asked curiously.

"I was telling them the truth about capitalism and the great and democratic America," she responded. "Maybe I shouldn't have done that," she added, as if talking to herself. "No," she pulled herself together, "I did nothing wrong. I stuck to the truth, and I told that truth to the young students. They need to know where they live, and I don't regret it. I will bear the consequences. Whatever will be, I am ready."

"What can we do?" another prisoner submissively asked. "There is not much we can do, surely not from here."

"We will see about that," replied Olga.

10.

Carl came back home, expecting to see Olga at the entrance and already anticipating her embrace, but Olga didn't appear. "Mom, Mom!" he cried. "Where is Olga? Isn't she feeling well? Is she sleeping?" he asked with great concern.

"I don't know, son," she replied. "I don't know what happened. She went to the market hours ago, and still hasn't returned. I didn't want to tell you anything, because I am afraid of the worst. I don't know what happened, but I have a bad feeling."

"I want Mommy!" Nikko cried to his grandma. Carl stood in front of the window, looking towards the marketplace and hoping to see Olga walking home.

"She can't be looking for potatoes for so long," he said to himself, and started calling every hospital in town, none of which could tell him what he wanted to hear.

Nikko refused to fall asleep, and kept crying and calling out, "Mommy! Mommy! I want Mommy!"

Carl tried to calm him down, even though he was terrified and uneasy himself.

"I want Mommy to tell me the story about the horses," Nikko continued crying.

"Mommy will return, my child," Carl told him. "She will return, so you go to sleep, and in the morning she will tell you a story. I promise."

So the days passed, but Olga didn't return. Carl didn't lose hope and continued to call the police every day. "I find it hard to believe that she is still in the country," said the Chief of Police to Carl. "Could it be that she decided to leave you?" he asked, apologizing at the same time. "Everything can happen in life, Carl. I am sorry to tell you this, but there can be no other reason for her absence."

"Well, it's possible she has been kidnapped," Carl corrected him.

"You know what?" responded the commander. "Let me make some phone calls to Leningrad. We may have a lead here."

Carl was pacing back and forth restlessly, from one end of the room to the other. He could not understand what could be the reason behind Olga's disappearance. "But why?" he asked himself. "What would the Russians—no, it cannot be! I can't accept that. I must go out and look for her. What would they want from her?"

A phone ring awakened Carl from his thoughts, and the voice of the foreign minister was heard on the other side. "I am afraid your Olga is no longer inside the borders of our country."

"Could it be another provocation of the Beria and Stalin regime?" asked Carl.

"I will speak to Beria," answered the minister, and at that very second gave an order to his deputy to find out whether there was a chance that Olga had been kidnapped by the KGB. "Give me a minute and I will check that lead," the minister said as he hung up the phone. He tried calling Beria, and after many attempts he managed to get ahold of him.

"We have a very special case in Helsinki," the minister told Beria. "This case is very delicate and unfortunate. I am asking you to check in Leningrad, and find out whether you have any information about a girl named Olga."

"Which Olga?" answered Beria.

"Olga Philipova," the minister continued. "I assume that she entered Russia recently. I don't have a lot of information about her, but I do have a personal relationship with her family, and I am very interested in what has become of her. In light of our relationship, we have to prevent anything bad, of any kind, to happen to her."

"Put all worries aside," Beria answered. "I will immediately give the order to find out all I can about the young girl named Olga Philipova." After a few hours, a telegram arrived at the foreign minister's bureau from Beria, stating:

"Dear Foreign Minister,

After an examination, we haven't found, unfortunately, any girl that answers to the name of Olga Philipova, or any similar name. We didn't find a case that is similar to what you have described, either.

I am deeply sorry."

The foreign minister seemed disappointed by the telegram. He called Carl and passed the news to him. Carl didn't accept Beria's words well, and decided without further delay to go to Leningrad himself. He said goodbye to his parents and to his son and began to make his way.

While Carl was on his way to Leningrad, Olga and the other prisoners in the cell were thinking of a way to contact Stalin. "I am sure he can help us, but the question is how to get to him," wondered Olga out loud. "Stalin is known to be the Father of all the Nations. I am sure he will understand the situation."

"If we could, we would have written him a letter," one of the prisoners said to Olga.

"Exactly. This is what we are going to do. What we need now is only a pencil and some paper," Olga stated.

"Hey, you," Olga called the prisoner that had been distributing food to the cells. "Could you bring me a pencil and some paper?" she asked. The prisoner ignored Olga's words, and closed the cell window in her face. "Why isn't she answering me? She is a prisoner in distress just like us," wondered Olga.

"What's wrong with you? Do you know what they will do to her if they find out about this? She is afraid, and I can understand her," responded the older prisoner.

Olga went on, "We have to find a way to notify the outside world what is going on here. I am sure that neither Stalin nor Beria are aware of the horror. We cannot just rot here in jail and allow these people to do as they please with us! We just can't!"

"Stalin and Beria?" the older prisoner raised an eyebrow. "You expect them to save you? I heard that Kuznetzov and Kirov are the ones who disagree with this policy of killing innocent people. Along with many senior communist officials who think like them, they understand that Stalin and Beria are murdering people to scare everyone, not to create justice. By doing so, millions of people have become robots, because everyone is afraid of them. They close the borders of the countries with an iron curtain. Europe, Asia, Japan, America and everyplace else. They think that by doing this, they are saving Russia from annihilation. Do you understand?"

"Olga Philipova," the voice of the guard was heard through the cell. Olga looked at him and the prisoners who were around her and wondered, not understanding what it was that he wanted from her. The guard interrupted her thoughts yelling, "Get out! Get out now!" he opened the cell, pulled her hand, pushed her to his room and made her stand in front of the wall. Olga's hands were tied and she was scared, not understanding how she could be rescued from this situation. The guard started feeling up all parts of her body, as if searching her. He was going up from the legs slowly, slowly, to her groin, paused for a few seconds, relishing the touch, and continued going up.

"Let me go, you creep," Olga dared to say, and then spat at him in the face. The guard wasn't bothered by her response and he continued to hold her breasts. He clung to her with his body and started breathing down her neck. Olga was trying to resist him, and she even changed her approach: "Please! Please stop it," but the guard didn't listen to her as he continued to enjoy her body. With one hand he was touching her breasts, and with the other her vagina. Olga's rage was rising, until she mustered all her strength, and pushed him away with her body. The guard fell to the floor, and was even bruised from the edge of the table in the corner of the room.

"You will pay for that, you whore. You will rot here in this prison. I will personally make sure that each and every one of us will fuck your brains out. After we are done with you, it will be my personal pleasure to kill you," he smiled cunningly and left.

"It is better to die than to sleep with a pig like you," Olga yelled. "You are not even human! Not you and not the others that are like you. You are worse than the Germans," she raised her voice.

Another investigator, a major, who came to the cell, chose to ignore Olga's outrage and started interrogating her, "So now tell me, how exactly did you escape from Leningrad? How did you manage to get to Helsinki in the middle of the war? Who helped you cross the border?" Olga kept silent, and the investigator continued, "I will give you some personal advice. If you tell me now everything you know, I will set you free. If you don't, you will be punished in such a way that will last for a lifetime."

"I have nothing to hide," Olga opened her mouth. "I crossed the border in a diplomatic car with my usual passport, together with my husband, Carl. There was no escape from anywhere. Major, let me go home to my husband and my son. I didn't do anything wrong, neither me nor my husband. We both fought against the Gestapo, and we even managed to beat them. My mom was killed in the operation for the liberation of the city." She stopped to catch her breath and continued, "We managed to break down the siege, and we saved the entire city from annihilation."

The investigator, unlike those who had come before him, listened to what she was saying. He was holding a phone in his hand and started dialing while she was still talking. "My friend, the general," he said to her.

On the phone, he said, "The situation with the prisoner Olga is pretty clear, and I have no more questions for her. She crossed the border without authorization by using the car from the Finnish embassy. I will tell you more than that," continued the investigator, as if he was Olga's defense attorney. "She married a builder with ties to senior government officials, and that is how she was really able to cross the border."

Hearing the words of the investigator, glimpses of hope appeared in Olga's mind, but as she heard more and more, she bit her lip. "We have all the material we need to accuse her of treason," said the investigator. Then she hung up the phone and said, "Do you realize you have betrayed Mother Russia?"

Olga was stunned at the sound of those words, but got her emotions under control, stood up and replied, "Now I understand that I truly betrayed Mother Russia, and I am asking that you execute me."

The investigator looked at her in amazement and then smiled, as if he had succeeded in breaking her spirit.

"As a faithful soldier, I fought against fascism," she continued, "and I can't just put an end to my life. Therefore, I am asking for the death penalty."

"Take her back," the investigator ordered the guards.

The same investigator who had been abusing her an hour ago knew very well where he was going to take Olga, and escorted her with a smile. When they reached the cell, he pushed her inside, but a moment before closing the iron bars, he let five more guards in with him. Four of them caught her legs and her hands and the fifth tore her underwear with pleasure.

"Help!" Olga cried out with all her force. "Help me, please, help!" The guards seemed to be laughing and continuing doing their thing. "Well, come on already! Quickly, get it over with, I want some too," one yelled to the other, who was enjoying raping Olga. When the second guard began, the other one kept calling him, "Well, what about you? Come on! What's wrong? Can't you get it up?"

"Who? Me?" he replied. "Sure I can, one second."

"Look at those legs, and that body! How can you not? What, are you impotent?" the guard's rage was rising. He left Olga, pulled his pants up, took a gun from his coat and shot him on the spot.

"You killed him?" one of the guards asked in amazement. "Good God, you are not only impotent, you are also a lunatic!"

"I am a lunatic?" he stood in front of everyone and answered. "Can't you see that the girl isn't breathing? It's like fucking a corpse, and you call me a lunatic?"

The guards were shocked, and while still holding Olga's legs and arms, they looked at him in shock. "Look, she really isn't moving! Wow, she isn't even breathing," one told the other.

The guard with the gun realized that he was right. Not thinking twice, he raised his weapon and shot the guards, killing them one by one. The gunpowder was in the air and the smell of death enveloped the cell. The guard straightened his clothes, closed the door and left the prison.

11.

Vladimir Lenin knew as well as Joseph Stalin did, that the idea of equal rights was a kind of deceit and fraud that could never be reached. As time went by, the corrupted groups only multiplied more and more. To ensure the status quo, they took advantage of innocent citizens in order to scare the entire world and to gain a totalitarian and civic victory. Lenin's indisputable approach was allegedly not to kill people by starvation, but by giving them access to only small quantities of food. Lenin assumed that if people weren't hungry and kept busy with trying to get more food, they would begin looking for nice clothes and luxuries. When they got everything they wanted, they would then demand fancy cars, and after fulfilling all of those dreams, they would go even further and expect social justice as well. He knew he would not be able to justify his horrendous actions. He would have no excuse for all the abominable acts of murder he had ordered against patriotic citizens who only wanted to build better lives for themselves.

There was a long line of people pacing outside the prison walls. Men, women and children, who were all dressed in rags. Wearing torn and dirty coats, they waited to visit their loved ones who were incarcerated within the silent walls of the prison. Just from looking at the red blocks outside of the prison, without even knowing they were meant for the prisoners, the anxiety of the prisoners could be understood. There were some who would come and wait for hours and hours, only on the slight chance that their relatives might be imprisoned there.

"I am only looking for my husband," one lady said with sorrow. "Is he here? Is my husband in this prison?" she asked one of the officers.

"Is that why you have been standing here for hours?" the officer asked. "It's a line that can last an entire day. Why did you come all the way up here? You can find out if your husband is here without standing in such a long line."

"We are looking for our family too," said two elderly people who had joined the conversation. "We came all the way here, because we couldn't get an answer from anyone else."

"I was in every prison in this city," said the lady to the old couple, "and no one is telling me what is going on. People have either disappeared or were arrested by the authorities, I don't know. How can we know which prison were they taken to? I don't even know if my husband is dead or alive."

The commotion began to grow, and the officer had to end the conversation to disperse the people. "Unfortunately, it's not enough that we have endured the fascist siege," said one old man. "It turns out that our government is also treating its citizens with the same level of cruelty. That is just horrible."

Among the masses, there was one man wearing a tie and polished khakis passing between everyone and listening to them. "That one, that's him! That's him, over there," the old man said as he pointed towards him. "The one with the tie is the one making all the propaganda against the government. He is the one who is saying they are worse than the Germans."

Let him in through the back door," the officer's voice sounded, ordering his men and pointing at the man in the khaki uniform. When he heard the old man's words, the man stopped and approached him saying, "I think I can help you so you don't need to stand in this huge line," he whispered and signaled him to follow. The old man didn't really understand what was going on, but he found himself entering the prison through the back door.

"What's on your mind, comrade?" the officer present in the investigation room turned to the old man and questioned softly. "What exactly displeases you?"

"I just want to know if my brother is in this prison or not. Why should I stand and wait in that huge line for that?"

"No problem," replied the officer while signaling the two guards with his eyes to come to him. His smile seemed to be that of a man who understood his job well. Several moments after leaving the room, meant to educate the old man in their ways, one of the guards reported with a smile that the citizen was too weak and when he fell, he was unable to get up.

"He is dead, Sir."

"Dead. Dead," the officer smiled back at him. "Go on. Transfer him to the room of the dead before someone comes looking for him and is liable to find him."

"It's 8 a.m. Reception begins. Who's in line?" asked the guard in charge of visitation. Each one in his turn, the crowd started entering the interrogation chamber, where two officers were sitting in front of a big desk that separated them from the visitors.

"What is the name of the prisoner?" the officer asked the first visitor in line.

"Makarov, Sir," he replied. "His name is Makarov."

The officer looked at his lists and then straight at the visitor, "I am sorry, but for his misconduct, I can't let you visit him. He doesn't deserve it. No visits or any other good thing."

"Why?" asked the visitor, while the officer ordered the guard to remove him from the room. "Pleeeeeeease! Let me see my son!" the visitor begged, but received no more than two deaf ears. Once he realized that he didn't stand a chance, he left.

The visitors kept entering the room one after the other, but they all left after several minutes with depressed expressions. The crowd outside saw and became sad as well, realizing that the chances of locating or visiting their relatives were slim to non-existent.

"This one is looking for her husband," whispered one of the officers to his friend, noticing the tall and beautiful girl standing at the door. The officer looked at her and invited her into the adjacent room. The girl was happy, assuming that in her case, luck was shining on her and she would be able to locate her husband. She followed him with a smile. They entered the room and he asked her to take her coat off, which seemed to her a civilized act. After no more than a few seconds, the officer's hands reached into her pink blouse. She grabbed his hand strongly and pushed him away from her.

"It doesn't become you, Commander," she said cautiously in order not to hurt her chances of seeing her husband.

"And I thought you wanted to see your husband," the officer answered with a pretend compassion. "No problem. You can keep waiting for another three, four or six months. I just wanted to help you."

He stopped as if he was expecting an answer, and looked passionately into her eyes. "You know that apart from you wasting precious time now, which is a shame, you are also dooming your husband's fate?" he asked. "Yes. Yes. You have the officer who is in charge of your husband's conditions right here in front of you. Who knows, maybe now, in light of your response, I will decide upon several days in solitary confinement, or I may add on several more years in prison. It's too bad."

The girl looked at him with disgust, understanding well her mistake in assuming that he would help her. She got up saying, "No problem, dear officer. I will go to the Soviet Union Attorney General, and you will pay for everything. I promise you."

She tried to open the door to leave, but it was locked. She tried to open it again and again, but to no avail.

"What's wrong?" the officer asked smiling. "Do you want to go out?"

She tried again to open the door, and when she failed once again, she started screaming, "Help! Help!"

The officer smiled and said, "Continue screaming—your voice excites me. You must have forgotten where you are, dear madam. Many people in here scream for help, but who helps them? And if you think that your husband doesn't scream, you are wrong. He screams very loudly too, but who will answer him? You need to understand that it is a prison, after all. Everyone is in distress. I understand that people like you object, but me and all the rest of us here are forced to make decisions, which in your case is fatal, you know."

"Help!" she ignored his words and kept screaming. "Please save me! Can anyone hear me?"

The officer kept smiling while informing her, "Look. You should know that if you keep it up, in cases like this, I will really be forced to make the decision to hand you over to the second rank of guards, who don't even think twice. They won't give you the opportunity you are getting from me. It's a shame. You can still walk out of here alive."

"Maybe it's an entire conspiracy here," she said, "and you are all covering for each other, but trust me that I can write a letter that will shock the Soviet Union Attorney General."

"You must not understand what it is I am trying to explain to you," responded the officer. "No one is going to believe your letters. This is a prison, love. No one is happy in prison. Everybody writes letters, because they are all frustrated, and they take out their rage on us. And that's fine. We are used to it, you know."

"I prefer to die and to maintain the honor of myself and my husband," she lowered her head and whispered as if to herself. "My husband is here for nothing, you know that?" She looked straight at him. "Do you know what he is in here for? I'll tell you. He, as an honest and smart man who has done nothing wrong to anyone, told the Chief of Police in Petrogradskaya, Leningrad that a policeman demanded a bribe from him. Now, when I see people like you here, I am really starting to understand what kind of government we really have. You are no less criminals than the Germans, and you will pay dearly for that. Each and every one of you. I promise you that. Even if I don't make it out alive, I promise you that someone will do justice to all of you, and you in particular."

The officer's rage was starting to build up, so he decided to teach her a lesson. He wanted to show her that he was not only threatening, but also executing. When he pushed a button in the cell, four tough guards immediately entered. "This girl assaulted me," he said with determination while pointing at her. The guards didn't think twice and took her away.

She tried to resist, but it was useless. The guards started beating her hard in every part of her body, until she lost consciousness. Then they carried her to an adjacent room, threw her on the bed and smiled with pleasure. "You always want to go first," said another guard, who decided that he will not be the first this time. He pushed the others aside and started making his way towards the girl himself, but the other two didn't give up and started hitting one another. There was a great commotion, which created a lot of noise in the cell.

The girl woke up and tried to sit up, but her body was too weak. When she realized she was naked, she started crying. She made a greater effort, and at a moment when the guards weren't paying attention, she managed to escape. She ran down the hall, looking for a way out and saw that the officer's room was open. She entered, took the coat that she had taken off earlier, and began to quietly sneak outside. The guards at the entrance looked at her, but they didn't know who she was and didn't notice she was barefoot. They opened the door, and she started running in the snow, refusing to believe what had just happened. She was running and crying for several blocks until her feet started bleeding. She slowly felt like her strength was leaving her, but she didn't rest and kept going. The extreme cold made her face turn blue and her body shiver, so she decided to take cover. Entering one of the buildings, she sat down in the stairwell, covering her feet with her coat and crying. She tried to warm herself, but after a few minutes, she passed out.

12.

Lieutenant Colonel Maximov was awarded a medal of bravery for his efforts in fighting to break the siege. After a long night of celebrating with his friends, he decided that it wouldn't be such a bad thing if he got to work late that morning. He slowly got up and stood in front of Vera's picture on the wall. "My beloved," he said and kissed the photo. "I'd like for you to be here with me. I miss you so much." Maximov enjoyed a few moments alone with Vera, then got dressed and went to work. He was going down the stairs in the building, still contemplating the pleasant memories he had of Vera, when suddenly, he saw a girl lying unconscious in front of him. "I wonder if anyone knows who she is?" he wondered. "Maybe she ran out on her husband? A pretty lady."

Maximov checked the woman's pulse and was happy to find that she was still alive. He ran back to the apartment, got some water, went back down to her and kept trying to wake her up. He splashed water on her face and called to her until she opened her eyes. As soon as she saw his uniform, she was in a panic. "Leave me alone! Let me go! I will press charges," she screamed from the top of her lungs. Maximov immediately understood that someone had hurt her.

"Don't be afraid. I won't do anything to you. Can you stand up?" he asked with compassion.

The girl tried to stand, but immediately fell back down. Maximov carried her in his arms back to his apartment, and called the doctor to get there as soon as possible. "I don't know who the girl is or what happened to her," Maximov told the doctor. "She has no clothes, no certificates and she only has a coat covering her. From what I can see, she should be urgently hospitalized."

The girl opened her eyes, looked at the doctor, and after seeing Maximov in his army uniform again, immediately fainted. The doctor examined her and checked her frozen feet. He asked Maximov to quickly get him some hot water. "She must have been in grave danger," said the doctor. Seeing Maximov's worried face, he added, "She can be stabilized. It'll be ok, but it's a good thing you called me."

While the doctor was taking care of her, people were continuing to enter the prison, wanting to visit their relatives. If they weren't allowed to see them, they left food and warm clothes for them.

"I just want to give him some bread and a few cigarettes. Can I?" asked a lady, who went to prison to visit her husband.

"No, you can't today," the guard at the entrance responded to her. "But if you'd like, give it to me and I'll pass it along."

"Can I visit my mother?" asked another visitor in line. "She was merely selling tobacco and got five years for that. She will be sent to Siberia soon, and all I am asking is to be allowed to give her some warm clothes so she won't freeze to death. Can I?"

"Don't worry. She won't freeze to death," responded the guard. "Give the clothes to me and I will pass them to her," he said and slammed the entrance door shut.

People were standing in line for hours without receiving answers. Once the reception office closed and the last ones returned to their homes, the prison commander summoned the guards to one of the rooms. Slowly, they started taking out all the things they received from the visitors that day. "I am taking the men's shirts and the socks," said the officer. "The rest you can take," as he turned to look at the happy guards.

"Thank you so much, Commander! Thank you," the soldiers responded while dividing the loot between themselves.

After taking all of the good items for themselves, one of the officers pointed to what was left and said, "These things we will give to the prisoners." He smiled and left the room.

The doctor worked to stabilize the girl's condition and Maximov stayed by her side. When she was awake, he would give her something to eat and to drink. When he felt her forehead to make sure she wasn't running a fever, his touch woke her up. Looking at him, she was afraid and covered herself with a blanket. She started crying again, but Maximov spoke softly to her, "Don't be afraid, sweetheart. I really won't do you any harm." He tried to make her feel secure and to believe in him, despite everything she must have been through. "I found you on the stairwell, and you were nearly frozen. But there was a doctor here who took care of you. I wanted to take you to the hospital, but he managed to stabilize your condition here, so you don't have to worry. You will be fine, I promise you."

The girl was still underneath the blanket, wondering whether Maximov was indeed telling the truth, or if it was just another manipulation against her. "My name is Maximov, and I am a lieutenant colonel," Maximov continued to try to reach her heart. "If you tell me your name, we can continue having a conversation. What do you say?" he asked with compassion.

Slowly, she removed the blanket from her face, looked into his eyes and said weakly, "I am Tatyana Pavlova, and I am an elementary school teacher."

"If I may ask," continued Maximov, "What happened to an elementary school teacher that she was found in such a condition on the staircase?"

Tatyana started crying, and it was difficult for her to speak. Maximov understood her condition and let her be. "I'll go look for something for her to eat. She has got to eat," he said to himself and ran to the kitchen. He saw there was a piece of chicken, and was thinking of making her some hot soup, but before he started, he went to the closet and took some warm clothes out.

"Take these and get dressed. They seem to be larger than your size, but they will keep you warm. I'll be right back."

Tatyana got dressed quickly, fearing that Maximov would come back and see her naked. She went to the bathroom, started to wash her face and stopped. She looked at the mirror, and was appalled to see the bruises and the beatings that made her face swollen, but the smell of the soup redirected her attention. Slowly, she began to believe she really was in a safe place. Maximov served her the soup with some bread, put it on the table and immediately went to make some tea too.

"I haven't eaten yet either," said Maximov as he served himself a bowl of soup too.

Tatyana was bemused and embarrassed when she started to eat, but then stopped. "I have a request for you," she stated as she looked at Maximov. "May I?"

"Certainly," he replied. "Tell me what's on your mind. What is your request?"

"I have no shoes to walk home with. Could you please go to my mother's house, which is not too far from here, and carefully explain to her that I need some personal items?" she asked.

"Don't you worry," he answered as he started clearing the dishes from the table. Moments later, he went out to fulfill her request.

Tatyana, who stayed at Maximov's house by herself, looked around curiously, and wondered who that man was who was helping her so much. She saw Vera's picture on the wall. "What a beautiful woman," she said to herself. She took the picture down to see what was written on it:

To my dear beloved, from Vera, your eternal love!

She looked at the picture and saw the woman, who was in an army uniform as well. "I wonder where she is?" Tatyana kept wondering. "Why is such a good man alone?" she asked herself as she continued looking around. She saw a medal, and took it in her hands with wonder. "He is a hero. A hero. What a wonderful man."

In the meantime, Maximov had reached Tatyana's house and was welcomed graciously by her mother. At Tatyana's request, Maximov carefully told her that she had had a minor incident; that she was robbed, and she needed a few clothes and some shoes. Upon hearing his words, as delicately and carefully as they may have been said, her mother became alarmed and asked to return with him. She quickly prepared all the items for Tatyana, and together they went back, walking and talking.

"I know she went to the prison in the morning, because she wanted to visit her husband," said the mother with worry. "What time did you find her, Comrade Lieutenant Colonel?"

"You can call me Maximov," he answered and smiled at her. "I found her in the morning, at about 11 a.m. It may have happened in prison, or after she left it, I don't know. You daughter didn't really want to tell me any details, so I respected her privacy."

Tatyana looked out the window in disbelief, "Mom, you're here!" She cried in excitement when she saw Maximov accompanying her mother, and ran towards them as if she didn't feel her pain.

"I will owe you my whole life," she told Maximov.

"What happened to you, daughter? Who could have taken your dress from you at 11 a.m.?" her mother asked.

Tatyana wanted to answer her, but she looked at Maximov. She was ashamed and not sure whether she should tell her the story in front of him. She looked back at her mother, and when she saw how scared she was, she began, "You know I left home at 6 a.m. to go visit the prison."

"That's right," her mother responded. "And then what happened?"

Tatyana turned her gaze to Maximov, but this time she thought she should share with him the information that was already known by her mother. "My husband was arrested for telling the police commander that a cop had demanded a bribe from him. They framed him with ludicrous charges, as if he had been caught for all sorts of lies," she said and looked back at her mother. "I was standing in line like a good girl, Mom. When my turn arrived, the officer called me in. At first I followed him, because I assumed I was on my way to seeing my husband."

Tatyana stopped her words, because she couldn't help it, but burst into tears again. Her mother kept holding her, trying to calm her down, and curious to hear what exactly happened there.

"I wouldn't go into the room with him," Tatyana continued when she was more relaxed. "I already started feeling that something wasn't quite right, and then four thug guards took me, beat me up and tore my dress from me. They all wanted to rape me," she cried. "You see, the guards were the ones who wanted to rape me, not the Germans, not the Nazis, our own Soviet soldiers!"

She stopped and looked into their eyes, wiped away the tears and continued, "When they started fighting between them who was going to go first, I decided to use that moment. I took the coat and ran. Since then, I must have fainted. I don't really remember what happened to me exactly, before I came here."

Maximov's face turned white. He couldn't believe what he was hearing. "How is that possible?" he asked himself. "Leningrad is known throughout the world as a city where the best and most honest people in the entire Soviet Union are living. And the army... how is it possible that the army that I serve in is made of such criminals?"

Tatyana's mother didn't leave her for a second and started crying with her. "Thank God you are OK, dear. Thank

God. And thank you, Commander Maximov." To Tatyana, she said, "Let's get dressed and go home. Everything will be fine," and she accompanied her to the bathroom.

13.

"Help, help" the guard's voice sounded as he crawled in the corridor, trying to get out and get to the prison guards. "They killed a prisoner and several guards," he whispered with what was left of his strength.

"What are you talking about?" asked the guard curiously.

"They... they wanted to rape the prisoner, and when they were fighting between themselves about who would go first, one of them shot everyone and escaped," he answered.

"Call a doctor to come immediately!" the guard yelled to his friend. "He will have a lot of work to do here, because he has to authorize other deaths as well."

While the guard ran towards the cell with other guards who heard the words of the wounded man, Olga was still lying on the table. She was completely naked and unconscious. "She has a pulse; she is still alive," said the doctor, who was shocked at her horrendous appearance.

"Who is this Maximov you keep calling?" he asked in an attempt to encourage her after he heard the words coming from her mouth.

"Am I alive?" she asked surprised. Looking at the doctor for several minutes, she found it hard to believe. "I told you I would not die so quickly, at least not before seeing Carl, my husband, and my dear son Nikko," she smiled triumphantly.

"Maximov is a close friend of my mother's and mine too, and I believe that he can save me. If I only knew where he is now."

"And from where do you know him?" continued the doctor.

"We fought together against the Germans and broke the siege," she answered proudly. "My mother was killed in that attack, and it's interesting that nobody cares about that after the war," Olga lowered her head.

"What do you mean? Why are you even here?" inquired the doctor.

"I am being accused of treason for marrying Carl, who is a foreign citizen," she replied, starting to raise her voice. "I married a brave soldier who fought with me against the Germans, and I am being accused for that, you see? And now, when I have a three-year-old son who is waiting for me at home, and who doesn't even know I am here in prison, I don't know what will become of me. Why do I deserve it? Can you explain it to me? Why?"

"I don't know why," the doctor responded and started to understand Olga and feel very sorry for her, "but I can look for this guy, Maximov, and let him know you are here."

Most of the girls had already been scattered to different prison cells, and the contact between them was only through aluminum cups banged on the walls. One morning, Olga woke up and saw in her cell, to her surprise, a pencil and some paper. She smiled at the prisoners that remained with her, and felt she was regaining her mental powers. With hope reinforcing her faith again, she told them, "I want us to keep looking for ways to inform everyone outside about what is going on here. Now, let's write a letter!" She took the paper and pencil in her hand and continued, "We will find justice. It cannot be that the world is not going to catch these cruel criminals."

"Dear Joseph Vissarionovich Stalin and Great Father of the Nations," the girls started dictating to Olga.

"Wait," one of the girls shouted. "I object to the title 'Father of the Nations.' He doesn't care about anyone."

"Is this how you talk about Stalin?" her cellmate jumped up. "He saved us from Hitler. He gave us food and water." She came close and thrust out her hand as if she was going to slap her. Olga pushed her hand away, while the rest of the girls remained silent.

"I don't think we should be fighting now," she said. "She is right in not believing the leadership of this country, and especially Stalin. But nevertheless, I think he must be informed about what people in uniform are doing here to veteran soldiers. We are all in this country either as slaves or prisoners in jail. It's unbelievable. Do you know what it's like in Finland?" Olga stopped and looked at everybody. "Among the neighbors of the Soviet Union, Finland is the only country that participated in the war and has managed to keep its independence throughout all these years. Against the will of the authorities here in the Soviet Union, I married a Finnish citizen. What do the authorities have to do with marriage? They wouldn't marry us here. Why does it bother them?"

"If they objected, then how did you marry?" her cellmate asked, while everyone listened curiously to her story.

"That's it—we went to Finland and we were married there," Olga continued. "It's a different world there. No one interrupts your work, no one interferes with you earning your bread with dignity and with living your life freely. Don't get me wrong—people work hard there, no doubt about that, but they feel secure. You can see that. It's different from here. Here, they put you in jail for life for nothing. That's why she is right, and we can't trust Stalin or the others. Unfortunately, we are all in serious trouble, and we have no idea who is going to help us and when. It's unknown, but let us not lose hope." Olga stood up, took note of the girls' alertness and continued, "If we are strong, and if we don't surrender, we will be able to fight for our existence. We have to be together and to believe, and maybe we will be able to win another cruel war on freedom." A round of applause stopped Olga's speech, with the girls standing on their feet and honoring her.

"We will not surrender!" the girls started together. "We will fight for what we believe. You are the best, Olga."

While the girls felt secure and hugged one another, in the corner of the cell there was a beautiful prisoner who was sitting and crying. Her long black hair hung limply on her shoulders, and her big eyes filled with tears. "After they killed my father, I am sure that no matter how much you plan, they will eventually kill me too. I know that."

"Why do you talk like that?" Olga went to her and started caressing her face. "You'll see, we'll write a letter, and when it reaches the Kremlin, Stalin will issue an order to release us all. Wait and see," she tried to calm her down. "And besides, don't forget that you are sitting here for nothing, and there is no reason anything should happen to you after Stalin knows what you have been through. You are innocent, after all!"

"My father was innocent too," she replied, unable to stop her tears. "His only sin was being rich, you see? My father was a smart man. He became rich during the period of the New Economic Policy (NEP), when Lenin allowed citizens to live better lives. But Stalin, oh Stalin, I am not sure about him at all."

"She is right," one of the prisoners commented. "The truth is that I am very skeptical too."

"I have experienced it myself," she continued. "When Stalin saw that my father and others like him were enjoying a good life, he decided to put an end to that, for no reason. In our family, everybody knew Stalin was jealous of people's talents, and even more so if they were rich. My father, for example, was immediately marked, because he was rich and successful. At first, he was arrested for some unknown charge, and a short while later they just killed him." The atmosphere in the cell went from happiness to despair. Olga didn't know what she should do in order to not lose hope.

"I don't have a reason to wait to be released, like you think," continued the prisoner. "I want to die and that's that!"

Olga handed her a glass of water. After taking one sip, she got up, and without being able to predict her next move, she slammed her head against the entrance door, fainted and fell. They all jumped from their places, scared at the large amount of blood that was coming out of her head, and tried to revive her.

"Help! Help!" they screamed to the prison guards for more than an hour. Finally, the slow steps of the guards were heard walking towards the cell. The prison commander, who was in the lead, walked calmly as he was joking with them.

"What has happened?" he asked the girls cynically, opening the cell. Seeing the prisoner lying dead on the floor, he continued, "Am I to understand that you killed her? Which one of you did it? Was it you?" he turned to look at Olga, pointing at her. Olga was not able to contain herself anymore, and at the precise moment when he was not paying attention, she attacked him, took his weapon and stood erect before him. All the girls were at her side, ready to back her up whatever the price was.

"You were the ones who killed her, you murderers! All of you! Do you understand?" she spat towards him and the prison guards by his side, with the weapon ready and pointing towards them. I would enjoy killing your commander first, since I have nothing to lose."

The prison guards started to back off, but one of them managed to sneak outside and call the commander of the unit to tell him, "The commander of the prison is in the hands of the prisoners!"

"Calm down!" the commander ordered him on the other side of the line. "Get back inside. Give them two warnings and call on them to surrender. If they don't, finish them off!"

"Yes, exactly. You are right, finish them off, but the commander is in their hands. They will kill him because they have nothing to lose, you see?" he answered.

"Kill him, you say? Let them kill him," he replied. "We'll find another commander, a better one. We'll find one who doesn't easily fall into the hands of the enemies of the people."

The guard, surprised by the commander's reaction, ended the conversation and hung up the phone. He prepared to send out an order for young soldiers, who were given special training in killing in cold blood, without showing any mercy.

"We will not surrender until we get an answer from Stalin. We have already written everything to him in a letter," Olga called towards the commander of the prison, still holding the gun in front of him.

"What letter are you talking about? There is no letter," responded the commander. Despite Olga's threats, he stood erect and was confident that in a few moments the menacing scenes would end.

"Stalin does not deal with treacherous prisoners. He has serious business to attend to, much more important than some letter by a few criminals."

"The army is ready for action," was the cry heard from outside the cell. Several seconds later, the door was broken and the soldiers managed to neutralize Olga and to catch all the girls.

"Put them all in the dungeon!" the new commander shouted at them. He had been appointed only minutes before, immediately after the officer's conversation with the commander of the unit. "No light and no food either," he continued. "They need to understand that you don't play games with us."

After the girls spent a month in the pitch-black dungeon, the new commander decided to return them to their cells. "Throw Olga into the cell of the murderers. They will do the job and kill her already," he ordered. He watched the girls leave the dungeon as they struggled when facing the light for the first time. Olga tried to remain calm, not knowing what could possibly give her the strength to go on. She could only cling to the thought that her son was waiting for her at home.

As soon as she was pushed into the cell, the murderous prisoners started touching her and caressing her body parts. "I warn you!" Olga shouted at a prisoner who wouldn't let go of her. When she didn't respond to her, Olga jumped from her place, kicked her in the chest with both her legs and knocked her to the ground.

"Yeah? Who else wants to try?" she asked, making sure the prisoner on the floor remained lying there where she couldn't attack her again. The prisoners maintained total silence. No one dared to interfere, so Olga realized that they got the message and started making her bed.

"She was in the dungeon for a month," one of the prisoners whispered to another, after Olga had gone to sleep. "They say that she took the prison warden hostage. She is dangerous, don't belittle her."

"Look how red she is," the other prisoner pointed out. "She is shaking in her sleep—we have to do something." She got up and went towards her.

"She has a raging fever. What should we do?" she asked while going to the faucet. She dampened a rag and placed it on her forehead.

While they were both taking care of Olga during the night, another prisoner heard the conversation and realized that Olga's condition was bad. "We need someone like her here," she said. "Let me help. Only with a girl like that will we be able to rise against these barbarians here. Otherwise, we are all dead. That way, even if we die, at least we will die with dignity."

"Good morning," the officer who opened the door at dawn said. Olga woke up, not trying to hide the fact that she wasn't feeling well. She saw all the girls who were nursing her. They were even bringing her some food that was hidden in the cell.

"You, Olga," the officer called. "Come with me, and keep your hands to your back. We are going to trial." Olga got up off her bed, and trying to stabilize herself, she followed the officer towards the interrogation room.

"Do you still want to tell us that you were recruited by the Americans through your husband?" the investigator asked her.

"You are inventing stuff that doesn't exist and that never has existed," she answered. "It is time that you understand I had nothing to do with anyone in the world against my country, or against anyone else. Leave me alone. Let me go to my family; to my husband and to my son."

"Well, I can see you are not smart enough to confess, but only know that even without a confession on your part, we have enough material to leave you in prison for many years." Olga, after beginning to understand that nothing she could say would help her, stood up. "Ok, take her back to the cell," the investigator told the guard. "Let her rot for a few more months, and I will make sure she goes on trial."

In between the menacing concrete walls and wire fences, Olga was sitting in the Crucifix Prison for ten months. The best thing that could have served in her favor, after supposedly breaking the laws of the state, was a fair and just trial. On her way to court, Olga looked out the window of the car at the city she loved so dearly, for which she had fought, for which she had lost her mother, and for which she had risked her life. She enjoyed the look of the road, the streets and the people, which were seen over the Fantanka River, at the Hermitage Museum and on Neveski Prospect.

Accompanied by five policemen, the door was opened, and Olga was pushed into the courtroom.

14.

"Olga Philipova is accused of betraying the people and the State. She married a foreign citizen for espionage purposes. She escaped from the Soviet Union in 1945, but was immediately apprehended," the prosecutor summarized his claims to the Soviet court. The three judges, who were known to receive orders from senior ranks, sentenced Olga to twenty-five years in prison, with the possibility to appeal only within ten days.

"Noooooooooooo!" Olga screamed, tripped and lost consciousness.

"Honorable Judge," the secretary called out while Olga was lying on the floor. The judge was trying to continue to the next case when she said, "You have a slight error in the name of the prisoner."

"What difference does it make?" the judge replied with a question. "They all go to jail for 25 years. Today's forms are ready and signed. Besides, who is going to remember her?"

"Oh, Mommy," Olga woke up and looked at the sky. "It's a good thing that you can't see what our brothers in Leningrad are doing to me. The way they behave after we risked our own lives fighting the Germans." Olga was sobbing and the guards were dragging her back to prison. "Why did you do it to me?" Olga continued speaking as if to her mother. "You left me here alone. Am I so cursed that I can't manage at any time?"

The guards were dragging Olga outside, and the judges in court were continuing to hand down sentences incessantly, not even looking at the faces of the condemned. They briskly looked at the listings and ruled. Twenty-two prisoners were sentenced to twenty-five years in prison on that day.

The Stolipin train, which was waiting for the prisoners, was divided into sections, and in every section there were half-cells with separating nets. In each cell there was room for six people, but that didn't really interest the guards, who were walking around like search dogs; they put at least ten prisoners in each cell. The sight was horrendous. The guards were running around with machine guns, as if fighting against the Nazis.

"Let's go," called one of the officers into the cell in which Olga was put. "I want each one to push his or her head to the net, so we can count you, and watch out whoever doesn't."

"At least I got to go out from jail and get some fresh air," Olga said to herself, trying to find some kind of consolation in her life. "I was able to breathe some air."

"Where are we going?" Olga asked the guard who stood in front of her.

"Towards death," he responded to her. "You will all die."

As the train started moving, Olga kept talking to herself, as if saying one last prayer. Just like her, all the girls were mumbling to themselves, when suddenly, one of them grabbed the net with her fingers, and was hit by a strong blow from the handle of a gun. "If you get smart," the guard called, "you will be beaten some more." At the sight of the prisoner's bleeding fingers, the rage of the other prisoners grew and within seconds they all started climbing the nets and screaming, "Murderers! You have no mercy. You are just killers!"

"Come," called one of the tough prisoners, while getting closer to the net. She took off her skirt and underwear and began screaming, "Come tread on us. Are you playing it tough? Come here, you shitty asshole. Are you playing it hardball while us ladies are locked up on this train?" Hearing the screams, the commander of the car approached them. He was a huge blond, and with his hands behind his back, he looked like a predator.

He was looking around him when one of the prisoners yelled, "What are you looking at, you asshole? Come cling to me, you nothing. That's what you want to do to pass the time on this ride, isn't it?"

The commander stopped next to the naked girl, not quite understanding her audacity, but admiring her body. "Tell her to get dressed and put her in my cell," he commanded one of the guards."

Of course," he answered while looking him straight in the eyes, "but I want some too! Can I?"

"Sure," the commander answered with a smile. "This girl wants it, and the more the merrier."

"I am hungry for a man!" she said entering his room while she began to take her clothes off. The commander didn't even have time to take his boots off, because the girl jumped him and lay on top him. "More, more!" her lusty screams were heard. "I want it many times."

"I'm sorry," he said. "I can't anymore, but don't worry. You will get more right away." He got up, got dressed and opened the cabin door. The guard who was waiting was unable to ignore the girl's loud moans, and smiled showing that he could no longer wait for his turn to come.

"She wants plenty, like you heard," the commander smiled at the soldier, and gave him the key. "Give it back to me when you finish with her."

"You can continue with him," he looked towards the girl with a smile, patting her bottom once more. The soldier entered enthusiastically, and then another one followed him, and another one, and another one, until she remained in the cell for a long time. Four soldiers at the end of the car seemed to be staring at the cabin, which was usually used for punishment. Seeing a girl alone there, they went towards her. "What are you here for?" one of them asked. "Are you being punished?"

"Do I have to be punished?" she replied. "No, I don't have to be punished. I am a woman, in the fullest sense of the word. Tell me soldier," she continued, "do you find me beautiful? Do you desire me?"

"For me you are nothing but a prisoner," the soldier answered surprised. Seeing his shyness, the girl lifted her skirt again from the other side of the net, trying to boldly seduce him and pull him towards her. It was a known fact that the soldiers were lonely. They worked hard, and barely got to see women at all.

"Do you have a key?" she asked.

"No, I don't," he answered trying to ignore her beautiful legs.

"Go ask your commander for one," she suggested.

"That is impossible. I'm sorry."

The prisoner clung to the net, pulled the soldier towards her and started kissing him. The soldier, who could no longer control himself, got carried away and kissed her back with great passion. With great resolve, she unzipped his pants. With one hand she started touching his organ, and with the other she took down her underwear, clung to the net and inserted his member into her. "Yes! More! More!" she started screaming. "Great! You are great! Great. Yessss!"

The prisoners heard the girl's screams and envied her audacity, for most of them had left their dear ones at home, and it was hard for them to loosen up like her and sleep with other men.

When the soldier finished, he zipped his pants, went to the kitchen and after several minutes, he returned to the cell and gave her water and dark bread through the net, as a gesture of gratitude.

15.

Morning came, and the guards took the prisoners to the bathroom to wash their faces. Each one had a small portion of food waiting for her for that day, which included 300 grams of dark bread, a teaspoon of sugar wrapped in paper and one herring. Usually at that point, in order to keep their calm, the prisoners would burst into singing:

"Horseman, don't rush the horses, I have no one to love anymore..."

Hearing the moving words of the song, both the prisoners as well as the guards would shed a tear.

The train stopped.

When she saw the shy soldier whom she had seduced the night before, she asked from behind the bars, "So what was your name again?"

"Igor," he responded. "My name is Igor, and yours?"

"I'm Katya. It's nice to meet you," she smiled and took off her coat so he could see her body again.

"Igor, come here," was heard, which stopped him from enjoying Katya's body. It was the shift commander on the train. He had just finished a satiating breakfast, and he was shaven and clean.

"Yes, Commander," Igor said as he stood before him.

"Take that key, and go get me the prisoner from the last room."

Igor realized he was talking about Katya. Jealous, he remained speechless and stood there for several seconds. '

"Are you deaf? That's an order! Move it!" the commander scolded him.

"Yes, Sir," Igor responded, and started walking back towards Katya's cell, thinking to himself that now he would be able to enter Katya's room, and not just have sex with her through the bars. But on the other hand, he was angry at the commander for daring to lust after her. "She is mine," he said to himself.

Katya saw him coming close, and she happily stood up. Igor opened the cell door, and the two hugged as a pair of lovers. Igor laid her on the floor right away and did to her what he was dreaming of doing all night. "The commander asked me to bring you to him," he whispered in her ear. "He probably wants to sleep with you. What do you say?"

"You mean your commander wants to rape me, not sleep with me, yeah?" she responded. "But I want only you, my love, you, and no one else." Katya went out of the cell with Igor, handcuffed with her hands behind her back. She saw Olga out of the corner of her eye, stopped and looked at Igor and asked, "Can I tell my friend to start yelling with the rest of the girls, so they won't let your commander rape me?"

Igor, who was so enchanted with Katya, nodded silently.

"Olga, get ready! I am succeeding," she yelled and looked back at Igor on her way to the commander's room. "Igor, I'm afraid there is not going to be anyone to protect me in his room. I am sure he has thought about everything in advance and that he is going to rape me now," she said, looking sadly at Igor to maintain the image of an innocent victim.

"You are my first guy ever, and if your commander touches me, I'll die. And if I die, please don't forget me," she started crying, whether as part of the acting in front of Igor, or because her fear of the operation wasn't clear. Igor seemed tense and excited, ready and determined to save the woman he loved, who seemed to him to be so innocent and chaste. He accompanied Katya to the commander's room, and decided to implore him and tell him about the empathy he had for her. That way, he thought to himself, he would release her and allow her to get back to the cell.

While Igor was making plans in his mind, the commander saw him at the entrance, and immediately shoved him out of the way. Katya started to cry, and Igor couldn't contain himself. He went back and started hitting the commander with all his force, until he knocked him down. The commander was lying bruised and shocked by the soldier's actions. Igor stood on the side, holding his head and refusing to believe that he had been able to do such a thing to his commander in a moment of anger. "We have to run," Katya whispered to him, with a big smile in her heart. "Quickly Igor, quickly."

"But what about the soldiers outside?" Igor asked helpless.

"We have to tie them so they won't bother us," she replied. "Don't worry, the girls are going to do that. Come on, let's go!" Katya went to the cabinet, where the commander had the keys, took them out, held a hand out to Igor and pulled him outside.

"No, no way. Wait!" Igor stopped. "We can't release criminals. The girls here are serious felons. I will not release them." Igor stopped, looked in her eyes as a boy in love, and added, "Let's run away just the two of us. Leave them."

"They are my friends, Igor," she replied. "I don't want to escape without them."

Knocks on the door interrupted their conversation, as someone was calling the commander. "What will we do now?" Igor looked at her.

"Don't be nervous, my love," Katya assured him. We will tie him up too, or otherwise, you will get a severe punishment, called the death penalty. And that will be instead of living happily with me. Wait a minute, I'll take care of that."

Katya went to the door, opened it and signaled to Igor to wait for the guard in the corner. When the guard went inside, Igor jumped him, held his hands and knocked him to the floor. "Don't move," Igor ordered him and started tying his hands.

Katya immediately joined him and tied his legs. "Just in case, put a rag in his mouth," Katya told Igor, and called the next guard.

Within one hour, Katya and Igor managed to neutralize all the guards and relieve them of their weapons. One by one, they put them all into the "love" car, which was the last car on the train. Then they were able to open all the cells and release the women. The girls rejoiced. Their lost hope had been restored. "Silence, girls," Katya ordered, even though she was just as happy. "We still didn't finish our job. We have to release the last two cars from the train as quickly as possible"

Olga joined Katya and Igor and the three of them started racing towards the commander's room. With a few tools, they opened the rear door. Igor decided that as the only man in the group, he had to do something that would impress Katya with his masculinity. He jumped down and using his body, he released the cars from the train. They slowly stopped and were no longer attached. The joy was immense, and the three started moving between the cars and releasing all the girls. "Wait until we decide which way to go," Olga said and stopped the commotion. "I don't think we should go out. It's better for us to stay here where it's safe. We can't take risks."

Since Olga's words made sense, the girls all went back to the cars. "Let's go to the commander's room again," Katya suggested. "I guess we can find something there that will help us."

"That's right," Igor agreed with her, and couldn't help hugging her with his great love.

"What is that?" asked Sonya, another prisoner who joined the three with a map in her hands.

"I can't believe it!" Katya screamed with happiness, and took the map from Sonya's hands, attempting to read it. "This map is our insurance ticket," she continued "We will leave to the south towards the remote villages, and we'll see where we can go from there. What do you say, Olga?"

"It makes sense," she answered. "We'll have to walk 50 kilometers to the south. We will also have to watch out for people we meet on the way."

"Just so you know," the voice of another prisoner was heard during a moment of complete silence on the train, "that what just happened here now, the fact that we managed to be freed from these barbaric dogs, that is a miracle! And that is why we have to make it. I will not fall into their hands again. Over my dead body!"

"You are right," the girls called out in unison. "Over our dead bodies!"

"We have 14 rifles and 4 guns," said Igor, after counting the weapons they managed to take from the guards.

"So now we have to find 200 real men," Sonya joked.

"I have to stop for a second to tell you something," Olga said. "I want to thank you! We have two heroes here, without whom we wouldn't have been able to do it. Katya, Igor—thank you!" Olga looked into their eyes and continued, "Without you, we wouldn't be standing here now, and especially you, Igor. What you did was a tremendous act of bravery. Keep up the good work. Way to go!"

The girls applauded. Igor, embarrassed and happy, looked lovingly at Katya, stood on his feet, bowed and ordered them to follow him. "This is your road, ladies. Go south and may God help you. Katya and I will go north, but we have to get some money. Without money it'll be tough."

"You are right, Igor," Katya agreed. "If we don't find some money, we won't be able to survive. But how will we do it? Rob a bank? A train, maybe?"

"It's important to remember," Olga interrupted, "that we live at a time that not everyone has money. Maybe hidden criminals do..." She stopped a thought for a second and continued, "Girls, we are all strong. We have been in prison this long for nothing, and we are honest women. I suggest we scatter, and each will find her own road. Those who are afraid or are not confident enough, can join me or leave with a friend or two. That way, we will help each other."

"As a first step," Sonya said, "I suggest we all follow you, Olga, and then we'll see what we will do."

The sight of the group of girls marching forward seemed

like the exodus, but only with women. The line was long and the destination unknown, but there was great hope in the girls' hearts, who had already tasted happiness. Back home. Back to their families. Back to love.

16.

"200 prisoners and one soldier ran south," the voice of the general commander was heard on the radio of the reserve border patrol commander. "The order is to stall them in any way possible in order to take them back to prison. Whoever doesn't obey, will be put on trial for treason!"

"Wow," Pioter, the Cheka commander (who later became KGB), said to a soldier who was standing in front of him. "Do you know what is 200 prisoners?"

"Do you think I want to go looking for them?" he asked. "I don't. But I know we have to. Otherwise, we will be blamed for treason."

"But they are prisoners," the soldier responded. "I suppose they are criminals, and therefore may deserve to go to back to prison, right?"

"I'll tell you something," continued 50-year-old Pioter. "Without anyone hearing me. From what I have seen during all the years I have been serving in the army, I am sure most of the prisoners were condemned for no wrongdoing. Maybe they were just criticizing the government and got 25 years for nothing. You know that the Communist government brought only poverty to this country. Poverty and death. They are using the innocence of the people, who want to believe there will be social justice and that they will be able to live with dignity and not as slaves."

"So what is it that you are saying?" the soldier interrupted, "that we have a corrupt government?"

"What can I tell you," Pioter answered. "My grandfather, may he rest in peace, always said that he was hoping that his children and grandchildren would understand it and fight against it, but it didn't happen. Eventually, we all became afraid of them, and no one is really willing to go against them. That's why I support the prisoners who have managed to escape in this way, and according to my understanding, didn't spill any blood on the way either."

"To tell you the truth, I heard something like that too," said the soldier. "They say that the people in the villages think so, but I assumed that it was because they were primitive, and I didn't really want to believe it was true."

"Just so you know," Pioter refined his explanation. "I do believe that it is the people in the villages who are going to help the prisoners. Wait and see."

In the middle of the fascinating conversation, an old man walked over to them. With a stick in his hand, he was listening to the conversation. "My dear grandson," he said to Pioter. "Can I tell you something?"

"Sure, Grandpa Ivan," Pioter answered with respect, which he had for the elderly person he knew from the village.

"I want to tell you that I wish these girls an overwhelming victory against this cruel regime. Everybody knows it is made up of an assembly of liars. If it were possible, I'd like to join them myself and show my support. And you should know too, young man," he continued, turning to the soldier. "I am not the only one who thinks that. Many people in the villages here in this area would be prepared to risk their lives against this regime, and I am actually on my way to recruit men and women who will take part in this existential battle."

The girls kept going on their way, with Olga in the lead. She was stepping proudly, repelling the cold wind and the snow that could not be stopped with her body. "I think we should take a break," Olga said as she stopped the girls. "We have some food that we took from the train, so let's eat something, rest and then continue."

Between the bread and the herring, which Olga divided equally between everyone, one of the girls also took out sugar.

"I took it from the commander's room," she said smiling while holding up an entire bag of sugar. "Now we can have a sweet release!"

"And who wants the underwear of the prison commander?" Sonya smiled and pulled out several pairs from her bag. "You see? I took these from the commander's room, so all our needs would be met." A choir of laughter emerged, and Sonya preserved the joyous atmosphere with, "We may have big asses, but the commander's butt is twice as big."

"A big ass," Katya laughed, "but a small penis, like a rabbit's." She started tearing with laughter, and the rest followed.

"Well girls," Olga stood up. "After we have all laughed and eaten, we should go on. Only now, Sonya and I will walk several steps in front of you, so we are extra careful."

"Olga, look!" Sonya yelled when she saw a residential village in front of her.

"Duck, girls!" Olga responded loudly. "Like I said, Sonya and I will enter the village to check that we don't have a trap waiting for us there. If everything is fine, I will call for you."

"I can't do it anymore," one of the girls said as she fell. She was having trouble carrying all her belongings, but she was immediately supported by the others. The moments when they were asked to wait served her well, and after a few minutes, she pulled herself up and stood on her feet again.

"What's wrong with you, Olga?" Sonya pushed her, walking carefully between the houses in the village. "Why did you pull your weapon? There is no one here, except for the villagers."

"In the war it was also quiet, and then suddenly they shot at us," Olga responded, saddened for a moment and then embarrassed, remembering how her mother and Maximov went with her to free Carl. "Everything is fine," she said as she pulled herself together. "That's right. You are right, there is no danger here. Let's enter and try to talk to them. If they, for any reason, won't agree to have us, we'll continue to another village."

Olga knocked on the door of the first house, and by that time, the girls' expectation was great. A young man opened the door for them, smiling and inviting them inside as if he had been expecting them. "I am sorry it took me so long to open," said the lad. "Have you been waiting here long? Come, get inside. Grandpa Ivan told us you were on the way."

Sonya and Olga's eyes met, wondering who Grandpa Ivan was. "Dear girls," said the boy's mother as she came towards them with her partner. "Welcome, don't be afraid. There are only good people here."

When Olga saw the woman showing such sympathy for them, she felt safe enough to signal the other girls to join them. When she turned around, she saw a crowd of residents running towards them with hugs and kisses. "What a nice welcome," she said.

"We live in a small village here," the woman explained, "and we love people. Today there are already 800 residents in the village."

"And what do you live from?" Olga asked.

"We live from the land. We are shepherds, and we raise cattle here."

While the villagers were having a lively conversation with the girls, Carl was sitting at home in Helsinki, thinking of Olga and holding Nikko, who was already four-years-old, in his arms. "How did you disappear without leaving a trace like that? What are you going through right now?" Carl said to himself, with tears in his eyes. "Wait!" An idea came to his mind and he went to the phone. "Hello, Foreign Minister," Carl said. "I am calling to ask for your help again. I didn't call you for all this time, because I assumed I would find Olga on my own, but unfortunately I failed."

"Carl, my friend," the minister responded. "I did check again and again about information on Olga, because I wanted to give you good news, but when I realized what had happened, I chose to spare you the information. But now that you are calling, I am first of all happy to let you know that Olga is alive."

"Thank God," Carl's loud voice sounded, so much so that even Nikko started crying, startled by the scream. The maid immediately entered, understanding that Carl was upset, took Nikko and went out.

"Where is she? Where is my wife?"

"I am very sorry to inform you that your wife was arrested by the Russian army for American espionage."

"What?! What the hell are you talking about?" he demanded to know.

"Yes," the minister continued. "She was sentenced to 25 years in prison, and three months ago she was sent to Siberia."

"I don't believe it! That is not possible! What is going on here, Minister? What espionage? 25 years?"

"Wait, Carl. This isn't over yet," the minister interrupted him and continued. "After she was incarcerated on the train a month ago, we received information a few days ago that she escaped."

"This is the Olga I know. You see?" Carl managed to smile for a moment. "She is a survivor, a true fighter. My love. Well, and what is happening to her now?"

"Well, it's not that simple. She escaped and took 200 prisoners with her! The entire Russian army is looking for them right now, so you have to maintain a low profile, Carl. It's a very delicate issue, so focus your attention on your child and yourself. Let me check and find a way to help you. Goodbye," he said and hung up the phone.

The conversation was over, but Carl was so shocked that he kept holding the receiver, having a hard time believing what he had just heard. "I can't believe it's true!" he said to himself. "My Olga wasn't spying for anyone. I have no doubt about that at all. I believe it is the communists, who did it to her on purpose."

Carl turned on the radio, wanting to listen to the news, and praying for another piece of information. "I will find you, Love. I will turn the world upside down, and I will search for you my entire life," he kept saying to himself. "I am sure it's just a mistake and a conspiracy. The Soviets will understand that quickly and Olga will be back. Good God," he looked up and started praying, "Dear God, please help my wife wherever she is. You are the only one who knows she is innocent. Please help her get back home."

17.

Sheep's milk, meat and warm bread. Those were only some of the diversity of flavors that the villagers served to Olga and the other women, some of whom already seemed attached to tall and handsome country boys.

"What will we do about the authorities?" Olga asked Sonya. "This pleasure will not last forever, and the Russians will surely get here sometime."

"Wherever we run, they will find out," Sonya answered. "Let's not even think of it. They will come, we will fight, and the worst that can happen is that we will die."

"You are right about that. It is better to die than to fall into their hands again. They meant to take us to Siberia as it was, and we would have died there anyway. But we can't hide this information from the girls. Each one should decide about her own destiny."

Olga and Sonya decided to assemble all the girls and talk to them about the subject. The girls came, almost everyone holding hands with one of the village boys, except for Lena and others like her who found their way into the bushes to make love.

"I don't know what will become of me," Lena told the villager who became her partner. The man ignored her words and took off her clothes. Lena got carried away, and they started making love time after time. "What will happen if I get caught? You can get a severe punishment too." Lena said while looking into his eyes. She was worried, but he was continuing to enjoy and kiss every part of her body.

"Why should we get caught?" he asked. "We will run away from here together and live in another village. No one will know who you are. I have uncles and cousins in another village, and I will take you there." Lena's eyes opened up with amazement. "But on one condition," he continued smiling, "only if you keep making love to me all the time."

"You fool," she smiled. "I'm all yours."

"Can you all hear me?" Olga asked. Lena and her partner hurried to join the meeting, to listen to the news from Olga and Sonya. "We all understand the delicate situation," Olga started. "We can't underestimate the danger that is lurking around us. I think we should scatter, and each one should go her own way. Otherwise, we will all get caught and be killed. Each one has to think what is the best thing to do."

"I have nowhere to go," one of the girls raised her hands crying. "I have no one in the world. My entire family was killed in the war."

Olga went over to her, hugged her and continued, "Girls, we still have some more time. Think about it all of you. Tomorrow we will meet here and see how we progress."

"We still have some more time," Lena laughed. "These days may be our last."

"Stop talking like that," her partner scolded and hugged her.

The villagers organized a big party to entertain the girls that lasted till dawn with alcohol and dancing.

"Eventually, they will arrest them," Grandpa Ivan told the villagers, who were sitting with him in the adjacent room. "And when that happens, they will all get death sentences." He lowered his eyes and said, "They did nothing against the state, of that I am sure."

"So why were they arrested in the first place?" asked one of the villagers.

"Because they don't think like Stalin and his gang," he responded.

"We will not let these girls fall," another villager's voice was heard. "We are armed with rifles, and whoever comes will be properly welcomed. We have to protect them. They didn't steal, they didn't kill and they didn't rat on anyone either."

"Yes, we will fight for them," the villagers agreed. "There is only one thing that bothers me," said Grandpa Ivan. "Don't let them send the commander of the border police here."

"Why should it bother you?" asked one of the villagers.

"The commander of the border police is my grandson," he responded.

"Let's go, girls," Olga's last call was heard. "Whoever chooses to stay should come here. We are moving on."

Some of them came to say goodbye to Olga, and some followed Grandpa Ivan, who kept looking in front of him as well as behind, expecting to see police or soldiers. "We will not let them come near our houses," called one of the villagers, who joined the girls with a horse and two cows. "Cops! Cops!" he yelled immediately, when he saw uniformed men on the horizon. He jumped on his horse and passed between the girls to warn them.

"How many are they?" Grandpa Ivan asked.

"Many, many. Thirty, I think," he said.

"We have to hide the girls!" called out another one. "We will not give them a reason to start a war. We have a mission here, and we have to do it right."

As the policemen were approaching the village, Grandpa Ivan started directing some of the girls to nearby villages and others into the thick forest. "I know you can see us," called the police commander, who ordered his soldiers to lie down and to get their weapons ready. "I suggest you don't resist," he continued. "We only came to arrest the vicious criminals who betrayed our people, and if any villager resists, it's a shame, because we will kill him too."

Grandpa Ivan decided to go out to the commander. He opened the door to his house, to which he entered with some of the girls, and exited fearlessly. "What's wrong with you, Commander?" he asked. "Do you want there to be useless bloodshed?"

"What do you mean useless?" the commander scolded him. "Those are very dangerous prisoners we are talking about."

"You are wrong, Commander. There are no criminals here. I don't understand what it is you are talking about. Come, come inside, if you don't believe me. We don't like the police, that is true, but we don't fight against it. Come inside. We will take care of your horses."

Grandpa Ivan welcomed them inside. "Would you like something to drink?" he offered.

"Ha-ha!" The commander smiled at the sight of two women in Grandpa Ivan's house. "You dressed them up as villagers? What did you think? That I wouldn't recognize they are prisoners?"

"These are our own women," said Grandpa Ivan, trying to seem indifferent. "We didn't see any strangers here. We don't want strangers here either. Come in, go into all the houses and see for yourselves, we have nothing to hide."

"I think you are misleading us. Those whores!" one of the cops cried out to the commander.

"Woman, bring something for the guests for the road," Grandpa Ivan called to one of the women. She immediately took a 3-liter vodka bottle (Samogonka) from the cabinet and started to organize a table with glasses, bread and cheese.

The cops, who started searching between the houses, heard there was vodka and went back to the house. They drank themselves senseless, and after several hours decided that they had nothing there to look for anymore and left. "Take care of yourselves," the commander called to them and signaled the cops to follow him. At the sound of the horses' departing hooves, the girls who had been hiding in the rooms and in the bushes, came out. They were exhilarated and happy for being able to get a few more days of mercy. It was all thanks to the locals, but mostly to Grandpa Ivan.

18.

With a lustful smile, Sonya asked a local man who had been chasing after her for two months, "Do you want a kiss?" He stood in front of her, like a bear facing his prey, but didn't move. Like all the men in the village, he too was amazed anew each time he looked at her beautiful body. Many feared to get close to her, even though they knew that she would sleep with them for anything, whether it was a gift or a good payment. In some cases, she would do it for a piece of bread. Sonya was inviting him again, "Are you ashamed, Vasia? Come closer," she continued as she started taking off her dress. She was feeling hungry for sex, as if it was the first time. Sonya lay naked on the grass, with her eyes closed, but Vasia was embarrassed. He was excited and there was a blush on his face, but he didn't know what he should do in such a situation. Sonya opened her eyes and scolded him, "Why are you standing there? Come over here!" After taking a deep breath, Vasia jumped on Sonya. As he began kissing her, he slowly released the rope that was holding his pants.

"I love you so much," he whispered in her ear. He couldn't take his hands off of her.

After two months of being in the village, the prisoners had become part of the local scene. They helped on the farms, fed the cows, raised wheat and there were even some who chopped wood. For the males in the village, it was like one big party. In the evenings, they would all hang out together, singing and dancing.

"We would be so much happier if we knew we weren't being chased," Sonya whispered to Vasia, as they were lying naked on the grass, hugging and looking at the stars.

"I think I want to marry you," Vasia said.

"You think?" Sonya got up and acted surprised. "Yes. You will probably want me to meet your parents first." Sonya lowered her eyes.

"They will be proud of me, you'll see," he continued, when suddenly he noticed that Sonya was crying. "What's wrong, my beauty?"

"My parents were killed in the war," she cried "and even so, everyone is chasing me right now. How can we get married? It seems like a dream that can't come true."

"This is a dream. But it's a dream that will come true and become a reality. We will run far away from here, change our names, make a lot of babies and live happily ever after. The question is, are you ready?" Vasia answered.

Sonya looked in Vasia's eyes, and he started crying as well, but from happiness. "Vasia, I am ready to go with you, anywhere. But we must hurry. Let's do it quickly, before more policemen come and it will all be over. I don't want to lose you."

Even before she finished talking, Vasia stood and helped Sonya up. Quickly, the two started getting dressed and ran towards Vasia's house. They took a bag of potatoes and some clothes and prepared to leave. "I will also take this," Vasia said as he held a sharp knife.

"Sure," said Sonya, "but wait, how will we get to the train?"

"I have a horse, my beauty," Sonya smiled, happy for her good luck and mounted the horse. "Oh, Vasia," she wondered. "How will the horse get home?"

"Don't worry, this horse is as loyal as a woman. He will not let anyone touch him," Vasia assured her.

"Wait! I think we hurried too much! What about the girls?" Sonya remembered.

Vasia slowed the horse down. "They can get caught any moment, and what am I doing? Escaping!"

Vasia stopped the horse, turned towards her and held her face, saying, "Listen to me well, my dear. The girls would have done the same thing if they were you. I promise you. And besides, you have nothing to worry about, because I saw the way Olga was leading the group there. I'm sure she will find a solution, much faster than you think. Now, start taking care of yourself, OK?

"I don't even have an ID card! How do you expect them to let me pass?" she asked.

"And do you think that I would have brought you all the way here," Vasia smiled, "if I didn't think of that sooner? You look very much like my mother. I brought her ID card, and now it will be yours."

While Sonya was excited and understood, now more than ever, that she was on her way to freedom, she saw Olga sitting in the corner with the girls. Without anyone noticing, Sonya could see that she was shedding tears. "Why are you crying, Olga?" asked one of the girls, when she realized that Olga wasn't singing and had a sad face. "It's better we forget about our troubles for a little while. Smile, and come dance with me."

"I can't stop thinking about Carl and my Nikko. I don't have anyone else in this world," Olga cried on her shoulder.

"I understand, Olga. You know that every one of us carries a great load of suffering on her shoulders, but we can't let that destroy us. If you don't pull it together, you will not be able to see them again. Is that what you want?" she said to get Olga's attention. The harsh words resonated in Olga's mind, and she couldn't allow herself to be discouraged and become melancholy. Instead, she stood up, wiped her tears, and boldly announced, "Come on, girls. After laughing and having fun, it's time we start breaking up. There is no other choice. Each one has to take her own direction."

"But Olga," one of the girls interrupted her, sitting with her arms around a local man. "We are safe enough here. Let's stay here a little while longer, until things calm down."

"If we stay here, sweetheart," Olga responded, "they will kill all the villagers, not just us, and neither you nor I want that. The policemen are due to come here again at any moment. They have already searched the other villages. They are not stupid, and it won't take them long to realize that we are here."

"Olga is right," several of the girls chimed in.

"But we have nowhere to run," said one of the girls with a rifle in her hand. "Anywhere we go, they will reach us, and even if they don't, the wolves will surely eat us."

"We can't allow for a situation where the villagers are hurt because of us," Olga responded.

"The villagers are ready to fight them, and even die with us," remarked one of the girls. "They are entitled to have a say, so why not ask their opinions? Where is Grandpa Ivan, so we can speak to him?"

The atmosphere was starting to get tense. Grandpa Ivan was sitting in the corner, scratching his moustache and thinking. "There are almost a million people living in these villages today," he started speaking calmly, to create a calm and relaxed atmosphere. "There isn't a family here that hasn't lost someone during the war. And moreover, even people who wanted to live a simple and quiet life, and just had a cow or a pig in the yard, the Germans would come and take them away. If they dared to object, they would murder them in cold blood. We have been living here in constant fear of the communists for years. When the Germans came, we all thought that we had been saved; we quickly understood they were even more wicked, and they didn't want to destroy only the communists, but all of Russia. That's why we chose to oppose fascism with everything we have."

"Just so you know, Grandpa Ivan," Olga said as she decided that it was time to step in. "When we were still in prison, we sent a letter to Stalin, but we didn't really wait for an answer."

"I don't know what good that letter did you," Ivan answered. "We turned to Stalin many times too, and when we didn't receive any answer from him, we figured the letters simply weren't reaching him. Then we sent a local student who was studying in Moscow. He went to the central post office there, and sent him a letter via registered mail. Do you think we got a response? None."

"Why is that?" asked one of the girls. "This is our government. What is happening here, Grandpa Ivan, can you explain?"

"Unfortunately, people like us, who only want to live for our children, for some reason are considered to be dangerous for our government. If you want to survive, you must kill anyone who gets in your way."

Olga lifted her arms and said loudly, "With all due respect, I am not prepared to kill soldiers. We would rather die than have even one soldier killed because of us. They are only obeying orders, that's all."

"But Olga, if we don't kill them, they will kill us," commented one of the girls, who had remained silent until now.

"Don't worry," Olga calmed her. "We will personally go to Stalin, and tell him the truth about all the corrupt people who are lying to him. Those that take a milking cow from an innocent man, do it for their own stomach and not for the country."

"The train commander is in jail!" yelled one of the villagers, as soon as he heard the news. All the residents and the girls were curious and stood up at the sound of his words. "They took two trucks full of soldiers and they were ordered to fire, because they say you are dangerous and that you took a lot of weapons from the train!"

"This is the time to move," Olga ordered the girls. Within a matter of moments, everyone started collecting their belongings. The locals organized a little food for the road for them, and they all said goodbye with bitter tears.

19.

"Run, Sonya, run!" Vasia yelled and pushed Sonya when he saw soldiers coming close to them. They were only eight kilometers from his cousin's village, but the soldiers spotted them. Vasia was caught, but Sonya was able to hide in the bushes, watching how the soldiers were trying to force his hand. He was resisting, struggling and succeeding in pushing some of them away.

"I was a soldier too," he screamed, "but not a pig like you." The commander became angry, and went towards him with a rifle in his hand, trying to beat him. Vasia grabbed the rifle, twisted it to the side, managed to take it in his hands and push him away.

"Put down your weapons or I will shoot!" Vasia yelled, directing the weapon towards the soldiers in front of him.

"No, Vasia. No!" Sonya cried and came out of the bushes.

When Vasia turned to look at Sonya, the soldier in front of him used the moment to shoot. "The woman is still here," yelled one of the soldiers, who heard Sonya from between the bushes, running as fast as she could, falling and getting up. Her clothes were already torn, and she left her shoes at the side of the road, so her feet were covered with bruises. Suddenly, she heard crying.

"Mommy, where are you? I want to come to you! I have no strength, and I want to die!"

Sonya identified Olga's voice, and immediately ran to her.

"Olga, Olga, I don't believe it, it's you!" she exclaimed.

"How did you get here?" asked Olga. "Where is Vasia?"

"They killed him, Olga." Sonya cried. "He was a real hero. He saved my life. He fought off the soldiers with his own body, and in the end they killed him."

"The world is a cruel place," Olga said to console her. "Much more wicked than we thought. It's sad for me to know that the criminals end up winning."

"Thank God you are with me now," Sonya said and hugged Olga, as both of them promised each other not to part.

Bathing in the river and sleeping lightly on the grass were pleasures the two of them adopted, until the cries of the wolves woke them. They jumped up quickly and went on their way. "Look, Sonya, train tracks," Olga yelled. The two ran quickly towards the train station, and came face to face with two policemen.

"IDs please," the police demanded, and then asked, "What do you have in the basket?"

"We are from the village," Olga answered. "We have some bread and cheese here, that's all."

"What village?" asked the policeman. The girls remained silent and didn't know what to say. "You are no country girls," he said. "You are only dressed like them. Come with me to the station right now. We have already arrested many girls like you. I know, you were all in the same village."

"Are these the dangerous prisoners?" the policeman asked his friend.

"Yes, tie their hands, so they won't run again. The train will come tomorrow and we will send them to Siberia."

Olga couldn't bear to hear his words. "It cannot be," she started crying. "We must be dreaming, this cannot be real. We can't find ourselves on this train again."

It was 5 a.m. when Olga and Sonya were thrown onto the train from which they ran away several months ago. They were sent to separate cells. The ride was long, and it felt like it would never end. "Soldier, I want some water," said one of the prisoners, who was as white as a wall.

"I have an order not to give water," responded the soldier. "I'm sorry."

"Why are you sorry?" his friend said. "They should be given poison, not water."

"Why are you talking like that?" the soldier asked.

"What why? Don't you know they betrayed the people and the State?" his friend continued.

"You are tough, eh? It's only water, and they are still humans," was the soldier's response.

"Yes, I'm tough, because there's no choice. We are trying to create communism, and these criminals are getting in our way. Until we eliminate all opponents, we will get nothing, you see? No bread in the shops, no sugar, salt, not even electricity or matches. What else does a man need?"

"By the time that happens, you will die," the prisoners laughed among themselves. "Without salt or electricity."

"You and Stalin both," yelled another prisoner. "We will all starve to death in the end. And I only hope you that you'll be the first." The soldier was getting angry, and raised his weapon to hit her.

"She is not worth it," his comrade remarked and took his weapon away. "You don't want to get into trouble for someone like that."

"I want to go to the bathroom, please," asked the prisoner who was lying next to Olga.

"There is no going to the bathroom now," the soldier replied. "It's only twice a day."

"I can't hold it anymore," the girl continued and screamed. "I'll wet my pants!"

"Shut up!" the soldier shouted at her. "You are not allowed to speak either."

"Yeah? And if I speak, what will you do to me?" she pushed.

"I will shut you up so that you will never be able to speak again," he threatened.

Olga was lying in the cell with her head against the net, listening to the conversation and keeping silent. "I wonder how you're going to shut me up," the prisoner said to continue taunting the soldier, in an attempt to unnerve him. The soldier approached with his weapon and hit her on the fingers.

"Ay!" the prisoner screamed. Olga felt she could no longer remain indifferent, and went to the girl.

"There is no use with these bastards," she tried to console her. "You can't educate them. They don't understand that our wonderful country is in a period of tyranny and great destruction. Do you get what is going on here? They either kill people or enslave them. These soldiers talk about sugar and about salt, and they don't understand that they won't get that either if we continue living under this government, under such oppression."

"There is a woman with a high fever," screamed another prisoner in the direction of the soldier that was standing outside of Olga's cell.

"There is no doctor here," the soldier answered indifferently. "This is not a sanitarium."

"What's going on here?" demanded the commander as he entered, walking towards the girls with his hands behind his back.

"There is a sick woman here," said the prisoner. "She might die."

"There is a sick prisoner here," corrected the soldier, and smiled towards his commander.

"We have no doctor on the train," answered the commander. "And if she dies, let her. We'll save 300 grams of bread," he grinned towards his soldiers.

The train stopped.

"Final station," a voice sounded through the public address system.

"The prisoners will walk from here to the camp," the commander clarified to his soldiers. "Take them out one by one, and pay attention that no one escapes."

The snow was piling up outside, and it was freezing cold. Large dogs accompanied all the prisoners, with the soldiers by their side armed with submachine guns. "Let's go," the officer said to the wardens. "Stand in rows, everyone. Whoever speaks or makes a wrong move, we won't think twice and she will die within seconds."

Supporting the prisoner by her side, Olga continued to march with the group of prisoners to the unknown location; two women in front of her who had already fallen and died. She was praying not to lose hope. "We have to survive,"

Olga continued repeating a mantra to herself. "We have to stay alive, stay alive, stay alive..."

The dogs were barking, and one by one, they saw the prisoners fall to their deaths. One of the youngest prisoners in the group left the row and stood in front of the soldiers asking, "Who wants to kill me? You are despicable, cowardly and lying men. I want to die, well, come on, let's see you shoot me." The soldiers stood silently, understanding that the girl was asking to be killed. "Well, why aren't you shooting, you dumb heads?" Only seconds later, a shot was fired into her skull. Two soldiers pulled her body towards a closed vehicle, which was already filled with the dead.

20.

Between Alaska and the Russian border, the Soviets built several camps, where they exiled people who were dangerous to them. Anyone who defied Stalin; scientists, intellectuals and military men (including the commoners who only spoke or insinuated something against the authorities) was arrested and sent to forced labor camps.

It was 6 a.m. when Olga woke up, searching for Sonya. She passed between the cells and saw girls who had not managed to make it through the night. "Where are we?" asked the prisoner that was lying next to her.

"I don't know exactly," she answered. "But I think that that this prison is in the neutral territory between Alaska and Russia. They say that a prison for the men is about twenty kilometers from our prison, and the entire elite of the Soviet Union is incarcerated there, including senior officials whose only sin was thinking a little differently."

"I heard there isn't even food here," one of the prisoners in the men's prison commented to another. "And there is another problem: there is no soap or towels either, and I am not prepared to give that up."

"I chop wood all day long, and I don't even get soap and a towel?" complained another prisoner in the men's camp. "How the hell can I get out of here?" he asked as he held his head while looking at his friends with a perplexed expression on his face.

"Let's send a letter to Beria. Maybe he will help us," another prisoner suggested.

"Who didn't we send letters to?" the first prisoner laughed. "We already sent letters to the general commander, and we sent them to Beria. We didn't get an answer from either one of them."

"And we won't either," a prisoner who was a mathematics professor joined the conversation. "I fought German Nazis for five years. I sacrificed my life as a loyal member of the communist party. And now what?"

"What were you arrested for?" someone down the line asked.

"I heard that Stalin was going to make millions from selling wheat, and we didn't have anything to eat. I merely told my friends that they shouldn't sell the wheat because people were hungry. Someone told on me, and I was arrested that very night. They wanted me to tell them exactly where I heard about the wheat, and when I didn't tell them, I got 25 years in prison. You see? And I'll tell you something else," continued the professor. "The friends I was sitting with when we discussed wheat weren't commoners. They were great people—Russian patriots."

"Well," one prisoner got up, sweating nervously. "That is why we were sent to a place that isn't even on the map and there is no chance anyone will find us. That's why we have to focus on our survival here. Are you aware that we have no soap? We have to protest and demand."

"Let's go, everyone into the cells," the warden in the women's prison ordered. All the women were still stunned from hearing the confidential information that came from one of the rats secretly cooperating with the male and female prisoner camps:

"The male and female labor camps are planning a strike to demand towels and soap!"

"Unbelievable," Olga said to herself. "We are talking about a revolution, and the men are talking about towels and soap."

"Funny, eh?" agreed her cellmate, who heard her mumbling.

"On second thought," said Olga, "they are right. Every day, I see people die, and it's safe to assume that some of them just got infected and couldn't survive. We are physically distant from the men, but we completely support them in the protest," she raised her voice.

A few days later, several kilometers away from the women's camp, an official announcement was received. The prisoners were going on strike, due to the growing fear of massive death due to lack of hygiene. "Prepare for a hunger strike! Everyone is asked to check how the situation is with the medications!" was called from the camp. The call had passed within a short period to three additional camps.

"We have to make sure the rats won't turn us in," Olga whispered to the girls.

"I really hope not," her friend answered, "but right now we have no way of knowing who is a snitch and who isn't around here. Yet, we do need enough time to prepare for the strike."

"Even if the Soviet headquarters kill us," the professor in the men's camp continued saying, "at least we will die healthy and with dignity, and not, God forbid, from cholera or dysentery. Who volunteers to run things?"

"I would be honored," called Petrov, an old prisoner who had been sentenced to twenty years. "I have experienced a few things with the people of our government leadership already, after exposing corruptions in the interior affairs ministry. I have nothing more to lose."

"What do you mean, experienced a few things?" asked the professor. "I wrote a letter to Stalin, complaining about Beria, who would give orders to put innocent people on trial".

"Ah, yeah? I wrote them too, but I didn't get an answer," replied Petrov. "I told him that they were scaring the people and the members of the justice system, and putting in jail innocent people who hadn't done anything wrong. But it turned out that they were all like a mafia there. Stalin passed the letter directly to Beria, and they all swiped it under the rug. But now is not the time for storytelling, we have to focus on our goal. We can't let people die from diseases here. We need to continue full speed ahead with the protest of our lives, and it is important that it is maintained in complete secrecy for now, until we plan everything carefully. None of the soldiers or the officers around us can hear even a hint on the matter. Is that clear?" he asked.

"Crystal clear," answered the professor. "I'll pass the message along."

Petrov gained great respect in the men's camp. They had all heard about him already. First, he asked for a meeting with the prison commander, who seemed like an intelligent man, a man that could be talked to. According to rumors, he had met with prisoners many times. Within several hours, two soldiers went to Petrov's cell and announced that his request was accepted, so he accompanied them to the prison commander's room. "Sit down, citizen Petrov," said the commander. "Tell me what is the deal with the strike you are so secretly organizing."

Petrov was amazed, and he couldn't understand how the commander had already heard about the strike. "It must be the snitches," he thought to himself. "They sure are fast!"

"I must warn you," the commander continued. "I heard you are a very smart person, and I am sure you will understand what I am about to tell you."

"I am listening, Commander," answered Petrov.

"I know you are responsible for this strike and it is important that you know that you are risking not only your own life, but also the lives of all the prisoners. I'll be honest with you and tell you that I tried to get you that damn soap, but I couldn't. They will not authorize it for me," he finished.

Petrov listened and nodded, stunned by the commander's candidness. "Citizen manager," Petrov looked straight in the commander's eyes. "I thank you for the conversation, and I even appreciate the efforts you have gone through for us. But it is important for you to know that we don't really have a choice. If there is no soap, people will continue to die in this prison, one after the other, and that is why we started the strike. So we either die of disease, or we starve to death."

"I understand," the commander nodded, "but I am merely the manager of the prison, and my abilities are also limited. I'm sorry," he concluded. "Take the prisoner to his cell," he ordered, "and then bring me the person in charge of the clinic immediately."

"If he is inviting the person in charge of the clinic after his talk with me, he must still be trying to do something," thought Petrov in his heart.

"This is the money that you deserve," the person in charge of the clinic handed over a large package of bills to the commander of the prison.

"Is that all?" wondered the commander.

"Yes, Commander. I sold all the medications that existed, but there were some "Bulldogs" who attacked me and took medications without paying. Commander, I have to tell you that there are many prisoners who are dying in camp, and without medicine, they will all die. They are already starting to ask where all the medications are, and I keep silent and I don't say anything. My relationship with you is more important, but you have to understand that the prisoners will find out eventually and they will kill me."

"No problem," the commander responded. "I understand you, and I will fix it. Go on."

The prisoners were waiting attentively for Petrov, who was seen walking out of the meeting with the commander. "Well, what did he say?" asked the mathematics professor.

"You won't believe it, but he knows everything. He knows about the strike and about the soap, he knows about the shortage in medications—he knows everything!" The prisoners remained silent. "But I understood there wasn't much he could do. We have to take care of ourselves and continue with our demands. Otherwise, we will all die,"

"The person in charge of the clinic is dead!" was the scream heard by one of the prisoners. He had gone to the clinic with his friend the following morning to ask for medications and saw the prisoner's body thrown at the entrance.

"Something stinks here," said one of the prisoners.

"No shit," answered Petrov. "It appears there is a conspiracy here."

Several kilometers from the men's prison, Olga and Svetlana turned to Masha, who was in charge of the women's clinic, hoping that she would give them something for the girl with the high fever. "Do you think Masha will help us?" Svetlana asked. "She makes a business out of it."

Politely and graciously, Olga and Svetlana tried to explain to Masha, an extremely obese woman who weighed at least 120 kg, that about half of the girls had high fevers and were too weak to stand up. "Please, Masha, you have to help us. Otherwise, we will all die," pleaded Olga.

"Exactly what kind of help are you asking for?" Masha scornfully asked them. "There isn't even any cotton in the clinic, and I have no medicine to give you. I can see that dozens of girls are dying here every day, but there is nothing that can be done. Now you are interfering with my work, so go away."

"What do you have to do in the clinic, if you have no supplies?" asked Svetlana, and fearlessly opened the medicine cabinet in her room. Masha immediately jumped up to her feet and went over to hit Svetlana. Olga grabbed Masha's hand and with all her weight, pinned her down on the floor. Masha started screaming and tried to fight, but

Olga and Svetlana were faster than her. They put a rag inside her mouth to silence her, and tied her arms and legs.

"I understand you want to die," Olga whispered in Masha's ear as she leaned over her. "If you allowed yourself to make a business with the drugs and let people die, I'm sure you knew we would come to kill you."

"Yes, she wants to die," Svetalna laughed. "Let's strangle her. She deserves it."

"No, no!" Masha tried to say. Olga pulled the rag out of her mouth. "Oh, wait," Masha moaned with real fear for her life. "I will give you the medications. I will give you a lot of medication and money too, just don't kill me! Please don't kill me!"

"Where is the medicine?" Olga asked.

"There is an opening in the floor here," Masha pointed to the corner of the room, "and there are different types of medications for every disease. There is also a large amount of money."

"There are millions here," Olga laughed, amazed to see two bags full of money and a huge supply of medicine.

"We have to let the bitch go," said Svetlana, as she carefully untied her legs. "I hope you understand," she said as she got close to Masha and looked her straight in the eyes, "that if you utter one word, we have many friends who will be happy to kill you." She pushed her throat until the last minute and then let go.

"Sure, sure," Masha whispered and coughed. A minute later, after she was able to catch her breath, she added, "If I turn you in, I will be sentenced to death because of the money."

"I see we understand each other," Olga patted her on the back and left.

21.

The rumor about the women's heroic action reached the men's prison. Pioter heard the report and ran to tell everyone that all the camps were ready to fight. "It's starting, friends. The battle is beginning. This is the time to demand soap and towels from the prison authorities, so they at least help us stay free from disease."

"The situation is not that simple," a prisoner in the camp interrupted. "The management of the prison already heard that we are organizing, even before we were prepared. The commanders disapprove."

"As far as I know," Pioter answered, "they approve now. Our demand, on the whole, is very modest, but you are right that the situation is a little complicated because of Moscow's reluctance. I heard that the general commander thinks we are a burden on the Soviet Union, and the only solution is to finish us off any way they can."

"That is unbelievable," more of the prisoners chimed in. "Our country wants to silence the entire world and terrorize us!"

"I doubt if any of us will ever be free to publish everything that is happening here," remarked another prisoner.

"We are on the way," Pioter continued. "All the prison camps are filled with innocent prisoners, who are civilians like you and me. They are worried for the future of this country and the future of the people who collaborate with Russia. It is our obligation to publish everything and to pass that knowledge to the entire world! Do you hear? For our future and the future of our children!" Applause stopped Pioter's speech. "I don't care what they do to me," he continued, standing up tall and ready for action. "I am willing to die in battle against the Iron Curtain. Against murderers, I am willing to risk my life in cold blood.

"I know that fifty men died in camp today alone. They were all young, including senior officers, army generals, scientists and professors. They all went to prison because they didn't cooperate with the authorities. We mustn't surrender!" he banged on the table. "Do you agree with me?"

"We agree!" everyone shouted and stood up.

"We will not surrender!" they all unanimously agreed.

While the applause mounted in the prisoner's cells, the commander and his gang were in a great panic. Some suggested that the commander let entire armies enter the camps to enforce order. Others, who were more moderate, recommended that he allow the situation to calm down on its own.

"If we turn to Moscow, to the General Commander, there will be an unnecessary mess," said Lieutenant Colonel Yusupov, who had been looking for reasons to replace the prison commander for a long time.

"When is it going to happen? The General Commander will notify Stalin and Beria, and then the prisoners will die. And we, the guards, will not avoid being severely punished for allowing the prisoners to reach this situation."

"I think it's going to be difficult for us to hide the prisoners' strike," said First Sergeant Bugrashov when he was granted permission to speak. "It doesn't mean that we are to blame. If we notified the authorities that the prisoners asked for soap and towels and we received a negative response, they have to know the results. It is not because of something we did because, after all, it was their decision."

"I think the prisoners are right," Sergeant Alex interrupted him. "If they don't get soap, they will die. They don't really have anything to lose."

"If we can stop Pioter, maybe we can neutralize the strike," said Lieutenant Colonel Yusupov. "I heard he has great influence there, and he is inciting the prisoners in the camps in his area. I suggest we put him in the dungeon right away."

While the officers were at the assembly of the prison management discussing ways to solve the situation, one of the senior officers came in and told them that the commander of the prison received a telegram. It stated that the Soviet Union Attorney General himself was expected to arrive and talk to the prisoners.

"I don't think that's a good thing," First Sergeant Bugrashov said to himself. "Too bad for the prisoners, because he can make a rash decision and kill them all. They are good people. They... But he didn't finish. Looking at Lieutenant Colonel Yusupov's face, he stopped himself, and didn't say another word.

"This is a fundamental mistake," Lieutenant Colonel Yusupov said loudly. "We have to get tractors into the camps and run over everyone. Only then, the Soviet Union will be able to progress for the people. Only then, will there be electricity, food, salt and even matches for everybody."

"You are right," his officer friends agreed with him, some wholeheartedly but others out of sheer respect.

"First of all, kill!" his deputy agreed. "Then, we'll see what happens."

"I don't support the commander either, for thinking that the prisoners should be treated with mercy," continued Lieutenant Colonel Yusupov. "These criminals need to die. We will talk to the General Commander in Moscow, and we will get them to understand that they are dangerous and that he shouldn't give them neither soap nor towels. Let them die."

"Pioter, Pioter," cried sergeant Alex, who left the assembly to warn Pioter and the other prisoners. "They want to kill you. Start thinking of how you are going to survive."

The rumor about the struggle had reached Sonya's women's camp. They were all talking about Olga and Svetlana's bravery, and Sonya was proud to tell the girls that she knew Olga. In the meantime, Olga, with a high fever, was continuing to search for Sonya. She and Svetlana moved between the prisoners, handed out medicines and asked everyone if they may have seen or heard something about Sonya, but unfortunately, she didn't get any satisfactory answers.

"Olga is a great woman," Sonya told her friends at the camp. "I knew she wouldn't give up. We are proud of her. Not only did she manage to stay alive, but she is also smart enough to be concerned for others."

"It's a good thing that we have someone like her," her friend answered. "I can imagine that she is saving many lives by what she is doing."

"The demonstration starts tomorrow morning," Olga called out at her camp, looking very weak. "Everyone is already prepared. From now on, we don't accept either food or drink. Only medicine."

"Olga, dear, you don't look well. Go get some rest," Svetlana pleaded.

"I have to see Nikko before I die," she answered back.

"Why are you talking like that? Stop it! You can't die, Miss Olga," Svetlana scolded her. "You have a child waiting for you, and you will see him very soon."

"How is it possible, Svetlana?" Olga was caught in a moment of weakness. "How is it possible that they behave this way to citizens of the Soviet Union? With all the optimism, there is a very big chance that I will never see him again. It's either I die, or I escape. Then maybe, just maybe, I'll have a small chance. I'm sure that he doesn't even call me Mommy," she kept crying.

"Let's go, guys! We have to organize. The General Commander should arrive from Moscow any moment to talk to us," Pioter's announced in the men's camp. A few minutes later, the General Commander entered, accompanied by high-ranking officers.

"We understand the situation," Pioter spoke as the prisoners' representative, "and we are prepared to accept what we have, but it is important that you know, Honorable Commander, that there are no murderers or spies among us. We deserve to live as human beings."

The General Commander seemed attentive, and the prisoners kept talking. Each one had his turn, telling about the sad situation they were in, the lack of food and the spreading of diseases. They told him that they had been prosecuted for no wrongdoing, and they expected a little bit of mercy from the respectable guest from Moscow.

"There aren't even any medications, General Commander," another prisoner yelled. "You may not know this, but the wardens here are selling our medicine."

"Honorable General Commander," called out Officer Yusupov, who was wearing his lieutenant colonel's uniform with a fancy hat and medals from his service, "I don't exactly know what this prisoner was sentenced for, but I can tell you the following: All the camps have prisoners who are professors and senior army officials, and who have been sentenced for severe punishment due to treason. They are the ones who are trying to incite the rest of the prisoners in order to find a way to defame the Soviet Union. I think this should be dealt with very seriously! No prisoners, no problems!"

"Well, I have heard your claims," the General Commander announced as he turned to look at the prisoners. "I'll think about it," were his final words as he walked away and left the prison.

Yusupov seemed pleased with the fact that the General Commander seemed to accept his opinion, and that the problem with the prisoners should be resolved as soon as possible without leaving any traces.

From the words and response of the General Commander, Pioter understood that the situation wasn't easy and preferred to reserve his optimism. He decided to join the

4,000 prisoners who, in rows of 50s, had been ordered to go to work; tired, hungry and sick. Sergeant Jamal received an order from Yusupov to get Pioter out of the row of prisoners and present him. The prison doors opened and the prisoners saw how Jamal held Pioter's arm tightly and took him out. Everyone began to understand that the situation was only getting worse, and that the conversation with the General Commander might not have been such a good idea.

"I am sick! I can't walk," Pioter begged for his life.

"Don't you have better excuses not to work?" Sergeant Jamal spat back at him. "Put him in the pit. For at least two weeks!" he ordered.

Pioter fell and was no longer able to get up. The guard lifted him to hit him, but Pioter had already fainted.

"Commander, he's dead," reported the guard.

"Slap him and he'll get up." Jamal said with anger. "Don't you know he's pretending?"

The guard did as Jamal ordered and slapped Pioter, shouting, "Get up! Right now, get up!"

The prisoners tried to get close enough to save Pioter, but they were immediately pushed away and beaten with sticks by the guards. "He's dead, and you will all die too," the guard yelled and continued beating Pioter with all his might. "You are not sick, you are traitors! Dangerous traitors!" he continued.

The General Commander left the men's camp and moved towards the women's camp. Olga, who had a high fever, decided to use the opportunity to tell him her personal story. "Honorable General Commander," she began. "What did I do wrong? After fighting the Nazis and losing my mother,

I only married a Finnish citizen. I committed no crime. I did not commit high treason. And it isn't only me. Look around you, at all these prisoners. They didn't do anything either. We know they want to kill us, or rather, to kill Russia.

"Show me one woman here who has been put on trial for theft or murder. You won't find anyone like that here," she continued. "There are intelligent women here, who have been sentenced only for expressing an opinion that this country's corrupt officials didn't like. We have all been thrown into this place, tens of thousands kilometers away, for many years. On this neutral ground, they are hiding all the patriotic victims of Russia, the innocent people, while they themselves are trying to cover their own crimes against humanity. This is the Soviet leadership that has barbarically been punishing Russia's elite. They only want to promote themselves at our expense. It's important you know that."

A round of wild applause stopped her speech. The prisoners seemed happy to have gained a representative with such eloquent verbal skills.

"I am not a judge," the General Commander answered without expression, "and this is not what I came here for. It's important that you know that your status here doesn't allow you to set any conditions. Higher-ranking officials decide what you deserve and what you don't, it's all according to the severity of the crime. And if you were sentenced for severe actions, you are getting severe punishments. If your conditions are hard, you can ask to discuss the conditions." From his response, it was clear to everyone that the situation was only going to get worse.

All hope disappeared from Olga's face, but in order to try to preserve the hygienic conditions, she went out with Svetlana to wash herself in cold water. "You are very beautiful," a prisoner said to Svetlana, impressed by her black hair and her long legs. She whispered something in her ear and stared at every part of her body. Svetlana was stunned and remained standing, frozen in place, as the prisoner started caressing her face, and then slowly descending to her breasts and started kissing her. After a minute, Svetlana gathered her strength, grabbed the prisoner, and squeezed her throat, strangling her. She fell to the ground, and Svetlana, even more stunned, didn't understand what had just occurred. She saw that she was naked, and looked at the prisoner who was lying dead on the floor. Then she turned to look at her two hands that had just strangled her.

"Olga, Olga!" called the voice of another prisoner. "Take Svetlana quickly! She is in serious trouble."

Olga pushed away the prisoners around her immediately and went to Svetlana. "What happened?" she asked as she hugged her with love. Svetlana was too shocked and unable to utter a word. "Don't worry, dear. Everything is going to fine," Olga assured, without really understanding what had happened. "Come on, get dressed." The stunned Svetlana didn't move.

"I hope it is clear to everyone that we haven't seen a thing of what just happened here a moment ago, right?" Olga told the girls.

22.

"Before we start killing off the female prisoners, we should help ourselves to the blonde and the brunette, shouldn't we?" Yusupov laughed in front of his soldiers.

"Today I want both of them together. Commander, can I?" Jamal asked.

"Sure," Yusupov agreed. "They are Olga Philipova and Svetlana. They are both beautiful, I agree with you. Take them into my room and enjoy. I am giving you the honor."

Four female guards, led by a very tall one, were called to Yusupov's room and ordered to secretly take the girls to Jamal.

"What is it?" asked Olga.

"You shut your mouth," the guard responded. "We will explain when we get there."

"There," the tall guard pointed to the girls as they went into Yusupov's room. "Who asked for them, if Yusupov's not here?"

Jamal smiled, "The commander wants to tell them a love story before..."

"Before what?" the guard asked.

"Come on," Jamal answered her, "You do know that we will all go home soon, because we will have nothing to do."

The guard grabbed her head with both her hands. "What?" she called surprised. "Are you going to kill the prisoners now too?"

Jamal didn't respond to her words, and concentrated on the thoughts of what he was going to do with the girls. "This cannot be happening," the guard said to herself. "We have to do something. We must notify Comrade Beria and Comrade Stalin. How did we become killers?" the guard said as she ran to tell the other guards what was going on. They were all in shock to hear her story.

"Maybe we can send a telegram to the party's bureau," suggested one of the guards. "He is the only one who can punish them for this plan."

While the guards started writing a letter to Stalin, Olga and Svetlana were wondering what was waiting for them in Commander Yusupov's room. "I wonder what he is up to," whispered Olga. "Maybe he wants to talk about the protest."

"No, I have a funny feeling," Svetlana answered. "I don't think he is a good and wise man who wants to help the prisoners. The girls are saying that he has already slept with several of them, and has also sexually abused them."

"What will we do?" asked Olga helplessly. "If he intends to rape us, I'd rather die than to give in to him."

"Me too. I'd rather be dead, than to have sex with that pig."

Olga went over to the closet that was adjacent to the window in Yusupov's room, trying to open the drawers to find something that would help them, but they were all locked. Suddenly, they heard Jamal's footsteps approaching. Olga whispered, "We have to open the drawers—there must be something we can use to protect ourselves."

Svetlana came to help her. They were fighting with all their strength until the top drawer opened. To their surprise, they saw a Walter gun, made in Germany. They looked at each other in astonishment. As Svetlana took the gun in her hands. Olga spotted a sheaf of pages in the drawer, written by Comrade Beria to Commander Yusupov, saying,

"I am bringing it to your attention that I have given an order to the General Commander, accepting your wise offer to wipe out a number of prisoner camps altogether, without leaving any evidence or trace, and to appoint you the commander of two out of five of the camps. This is after three of them will cease to exist.

A communist salute,

Signed, Comrade Beria

"I can't believe it, Svetlana," said Olga. "This letter was written by Beria himself! Do you get it? That means that Stalin knows about the murders of thousands of innocent people, and there are no mistakes as far as they are concerned."

"That means that Stalin himself is killing Russia!" Svetlana answered, still in shock. At the sound of Jamal's footsteps, she stood up, put the ammunition into the gun and hid her hands behind her back.

Yusupov went to his room too, and met Jamal on the way. "Allah is with you, Commander. Today you are going to have a double celebration."

"Why double?" Yusupov wondered, being in high spirits. "Once, for succeeding to convince the guest from Moscow to liquidate a number of camps and we will all go home, thanks to you, and twice, for being able to celebrate with the surprise that is waiting for you in your room. As I see it, you are my commander so you have the right to go first."

"Thank you, Jamal," Yusupov answered smiling before entering the room. "I will make sure to increase your rank and I will also increase your salary. Ah, and I'll also give you some girls for your pleasure."

"Salam Aleikum," Yusupov welcomed the girls as he opened the door to his room. "Please sit down, feel comfortable. You have good reason to feel happy today." Olga and Svetlana looked at each other but didn't say anything. "You must be asking yourselves why you are here. It's because I am in high spirits today, and I am the only one who can save you. If we stay friends, you will be able to save yourselves and remain alive."

"Excuse us," Olga interrupted him, "but what did we do to have the honor of coming to your room and receiving such a personal invitation from you?"

"Yes," Svetlana chimed in. "We find it very surprising that such an important and busy person like yourself invites us to his private room."

"Don't you understand that your lives depend on me? That I am the only one who has the ability to save you? In a few days, your camps will be liquidated. So, again, if you behave, I will be able to transfer you to another camp," he promised.

"We don't understand what this liquidation is, and what do you mean by behaving?" Olga asked innocently.

"I'll answer your second question," Yusupov said proudly. "I don't like seeing you in a prisoner's uniform, so as the first step, I want you to take them off. We are alone today, and I want you very badly."

Even though they already knew his intentions, Olga and Svetlana weren't expecting such directness and remained silent for a few seconds. "What don't you understand?" Yusupov raised his voice. "Take your prisoner uniforms off right now! Come on, girls, for it's clear to us all that it has been a while since you were fucked." The girls were still not moving. "I don't understand. Do you want me to put you both in the pit? Do you prefer the pit over a cock?"

"You first. You undress first," Olga decided to begin. "We will undress right after you."

"I understand, girls. You want to see my big dick, eh? That's fine," Yusupov answered, feeling flattered, and starting to take his shirt off. "Now you."

"We haven't seen anything yet. Take off your underwear too," Svetlana said. Yusupov obeyed her and stood naked and proud. "Well, what are you saying?"

"I thought you had a bigger tool," Svetlana expressed her disappointment. "For that, it's not worth it."

"For me too, it's just too small," Olga added, when Yusupov was already starting to lose his patience and went to get his clothes.

"Not so fast," Svetlana blocked his way. "We are not done with you yet."

"I'll kill you, you whore!" Yusupov shouted as he raised his hand, trying to push Svetlana away. Then she knocked him to the floor with one punch, pinning the gun to his head. Yusupov, already feeling helpless, changed his tone of speech and begged for his life. "Don't kill me, please! I have eight children. They are all small, and who will provide for them?"

"You should of thought of that before," answered Svetlana. "A long time before you decided to kill thousands of people. Now it's too late. We will execute you and hang you here, in the prison yard."

"But first, we owe him a little surgery," Olga interfered, looking at Svetlana. "What do you say? Should we cut off his penis and balls? That way, he won't have the desire to live anymore."

Yusupov's face turned white and he said, "I am begging you, don't do it to me. I can pay you a lot of money! Please."

"Where did your money come from?" Olga asked, stepping on his inflated belly with her foot and continuing. "Where from, eh? From selling the medications, or from killing hundreds of people? Svetlana, give me a few sheets please. I want to hang him as a traitor of the people and the Soviet Motherland. In the afterlife, he is going straight to hell, that's for sure."

"I will give you all the money," Yusupov kept crying and begging for his life. "I have a lot of money. Look for yourselves, the key is in my pocket pants. Please, let me live."

While Svetlana was standing with the gun directed at Yusupov's skull, Olga went over to his pants and took a key chain from them. She opened the drawer and found piles of money. "You asshole! You murdering prick! Where did you steal so much money from?" Olga came close to Yusupov and squeezed his throat with her hand. "Come on, speak! Where did all this money come from?"

"If I tell you, will you let me live?" he pleaded.

"Maybe," answered Olga, not letting go of his throat.

"You have a small chance to live, and maybe even remain in your position. Let's go, asshole. Where did you get so much money from?"

"Was it from killing the medicine man in the men's prison?" added Svetlana, and Yusupov started crying and slamming his head against the floor.

"Crying won't do you any good," Olga raised her voice, kicking him hard and tying both his legs with a sheet.

"He was threatening me," he started mumbling and crying bitter tears. "He wanted to rat me out, and so I killed him next to the clinic."

"OK. Now we are getting somewhere. Get up, sit at your desk and start writing the truth! After you are done, you will start writing a letter to the General Commander." Yusupov was shocked, but he obeyed Olga. Crying, and with his legs tied, he dragged himself to the table and started writing the truth in detail.

"Careful not to fake it," Svetlana said as she slapped his face. When he finished writing, Olga started untying the sheet from his legs.

"What about the gun?" asked Yusupov, while he was getting dressed and escorting them out. "You will get the gun in the afterlife," Olga responded, holding Svetlana's hand and running with her outside so they could bury the bucket of money in a safe place.

"Now we can go to sleep quietly," Svetlana said to sum up the experience. "We have enough money for medicines and for soap too."

2⃞.

Pioter and some of his friends were thrown into the pit for two weeks. The rumor about Stalin and Beria's order, of them wanting to kill all the prisoners, was slowly reaching everyone. In the men's prison, there was already great agitation. The prisoners stopped working, and demanded that Pioter and the others be released. "We are probably going to die," a prisoner stood on the table in the yard and told everyone. "It is important for the entire world to know under whose orders we are going to die! And for what? For soap and towels? No. Everyone has to know that soap is not the real reason. The truth is that we are going to be killed for being patriots of this country and for wanting to help it. No leadership will be able to hide these crimes from the free world, especially from the people of the Soviet Union. You'll see, the world will not forgive them. If not us, then our children will put them on trial."

In the women's prison, there was a great commotion. The prisoners were standing in front of the offices of the prison management and shouting curses at Stalin and his gang. In light of the protests in the camps, the General Commander and his friends arranged to meet the prison commanders.

"I can see you didn't have the brains to find a solution," the General Commander said, with his senior officers sitting around him in a circle. "What do you have to say about that, Comrade Bobrov? And you, Comrade Yusupov? What's the matter that you are so quiet now?"

"In the women's camp there are young girls that we can keep," answered Yusupov, lowering his eyes as the silence in the room became unbearably loud.

"I understand you need girls?" the commander laughed, and the rest of the men followed his lead. "They will eat you up alive. Do you have any idea with what dangerous women you are dealing with here?"

"I am against the murder of the prisoners," Commander Bobrov interrupted him.

"The minute the soldiers and the tractors get here, you will be taking orders from me," the General Commander remarked as he concluded the meeting and signaled his officers to follow him.

The atmosphere was bleak and gloomy, and there were a lot of disagreements. Commander Bobrov decided to go home, because he felt he could not bear the remainder of the day at the prison.

"I am not feeling well," Bobrov nestled in his wife's arms. "I never thought that the General Commander, with Stalin and Beria knowing, would come to kill prisoners in the prison. Can you believe it? I know they want to kill that prisoner in the men's camp who incites everyone on the issue of soap and towels, but from that to mass murder? I have never heard of such a thing."

"Many prisoners die from diseases, don't they?" his wife asked, when knocks on the door diverted the couple's attention.

"An officer is here," the wife said to Bobrov. "It's the prosecutor's assistant. He is asking to speak with you urgently, but you haven't eaten anything yet."

"It'll take a few minutes," Bobrov answered, kissed her and went out with the officer on his way. The rumor that the tractors were on the way to the camps was circulating, and everyone was aware that the General Commander was planning to begin his work in Camp Number One, and continue to the women's camp from there.

Pioter's mental condition, after being in the pit for two months, was deteriorating. He had been walking around like a wounded lion, not receiving letters or any signs of life from home. Yusupov's men even took the photos of his family, whom he hadn't seen for more than seven years. "What's the point in living in such a world," he wondered to himself. "Who can change a murderer's dictatorship? A man who takes the lives of all those that have a different opinion than him?"

Pioter stood in front of the door, dreaming that he was holding a key and being freed. In his imagination, he went to the Kremlin, to the private home of the Father of the Nations, Joseph Stalin, and started shooting with a gun without showing mercy. He was shooting and shooting, like he remembered shooting the Germans. He was unable to stop crying, saying, "This is for Michael! This is for Mark!" The sudden footsteps of the guards brought him back to reality. "Let's go, you are coming with us to the deputy commander of the prison. Hands behind your back!" the guards ordered him, and started walking out with him for all the prisoners to see.

"They are taking him out of prison," were the whispers heard everywhere. "I wonder where they are taking him."

"Move it already," the guard ordered, and pushed him forward towards the nearby forest. He was joking with his colleague in a language Pioter didn't understand. "Now stand still!" Said commanded. "When we shoot, you run straight forward, got it? Straight all the time, until you reach a village. I hope that there is someone there who will be able to help you."

Pioter looked at them, fearing more than ever for his fate. "Why are you in shock? Say thank you. We got an order to execute you, but we understand that they are exaggerating, so we decided not to comply with the order. Now scram. Go on," they told him.

Pioter couldn't believe their words. He still assumed that the minute he ran, they would shoot him. "Don't worry, we're in the same situation as you," the guard yelled at him, and started firing. "We don't like them either. Run already and don't look back. Go on, you are free, run!"

While Pioter managed to disappear in between the trees of the forest, it was as if his dream came true, while in the nearby camp, dozens of prisoners were awaiting their death. "I think that after they have taken Pioter, they will get back to us with a battalion of murderers with automatic weapons and take us all down," commented a prisoner named Felix, who feared for his life.

"What were you sentenced for?" his cellmate asked him.

"Ah... nonsense. I wrote a few poems about the old tyrant, Stalin, spread it among some friends and here I am for twenty years, you see?" he answered.

His friend identified with him. "We have to unite forces. They have no laws here."

"We cannot remain silent. I gave my life here for nothing," Felix continued, and when he could no longer hold his tears in, the other prisoners started crying with him.

"Is there anyone here that still doesn't believe that Stalin is the one who is giving these murderous orders?" called out one of the prisoners who stood up.

There was silence in the camp when an older man, who had been in jail since 1937, said quietly, "Excuse me, can I say something?" With everyone's eyes looking straight at him, he said, "I can't believe that Comrade Stalin is involved in such a cruel decision to kill the prisoners. It's hard for me to believe. I have been here for many years already, and I think that the decision might have been taken by the General Commander and his friends, but not Stalin. And anyway, I don't believe they will kill us without a trial. It seems that someone here is pulling the strings and trying to incite you all to take advantage of the situation and run. I'm sorry fellows, I will not participate in this mess. I'd rather wait it out. They did say several times already that we would be freed soon, so why spoil our last chance? I want to get home alive, and I am sure you do too. If we start fighting now, I'm sure we will all die, and no one will ever know what happened here.

"Shut the fuck up and wait to die like a dog?" another prisoner yelled at him. "I don't want to wait. There is no point in waiting! We have to break everything and run at whatever cost. Whatever the cost is, you hear?"

"Whatever the cost is! Whatever the cost is!" everyone called out together.

"I have to tell you another thing," Felix yelled, feeling more confident now, when he realized the sympathy around him. "Someone told me that in Moscow they are arresting doctors, mostly Jews, and Jewish professors who are known as specialists in the Soviet Union. They are arresting them because they spread a rumor that they harmed the patients on purpose. Do you understand that this is a serious blow to medicine and to the entire country? We have to start attacking from within!" Felix raised his voice. "Don't forget that they have already succeeded in the past, and the situation is much more delicate now, because they realize that we are starting to influence from within! Why do you think the General Commander from Moscow ordered the soldiers and the tractors to the prison? If we don't act immediately, we will all be in great danger, that is clear."

The prisoners started to argue with one another and tried to convince each other that they were right, while those that believed in Stalin and Beria were aggressively attacking Felix. "Who are you to state such facts? Stalin will never be an accomplice to genocide!" yelled one prisoner who was sure of Stalin and his way.

"Rhetoric," replied several old prisoners, who had a great effect among the prisoners and identified with Felix's words. Then one of the hotheaded prisoners jumped on Beria's oppose and started beating him with all the strength he had. The unrest in the camp was growing with one beating the other until it was hard to discern who was against whom.

While the riot in the men's camp was underway, Yusupov was depressed and sitting in his room in the women's camp. He felt his dignity had been destroyed by two young girls, who had managed to get enough solid proof to convict him.

2🔲.

Pioter was continuing to make his way through the Yakutia Forest when, to his surprise, he saw the yurts (guesthouses) in front of him. He tried to crawl towards them, pulling himself along, but after several moments he fainted and fell on the frozen ice. Locals who passed by saw him and rushed to his aid. In light of his condition, the residents lifted him, and with sledges meant for driving in the snow, they lead him to the nearest tent to help him.

"Where am I?" Pioter asked when he finally opened his eyes, looking towards the opening of the tent and seeing it is dark outside.

"Rest. Don't worry, you are in a safe place. We will not turn you in," a female standing near him said. The locals made their living from fishing, hunting and selling furs. The woman who answered him had by chance been fishing with her brother when they came across his half-frozen body.

At the sound of her friendly voice and the look of her slanted eyes, Pioter revived. He had not heard a woman's voice or seen a female figure for seven years, but he was too frail to get up and thank her. "Eat and go back to sleep. This is not the time to talk," she said as she put out some warm soup.

At dawn, Pioter woke up to a tray full of all kinds of tasty dishes. He devoured the food like a wolf that had never seen prey his whole life. He kept looking around him, thinking that someone might try to take it from him. The slant-eyed woman was sitting in front of him, smiling. "Thank you very much, lady," Pioter said as he looked into her warm eyes, which expressed empathy. "What is your name?"

"I am Valia," she responded.

"Thank you Valia. You are a very sexy woman, you know?" he said and put his hands on her fleshy legs. Valia, also feeling an intense sexual attraction to Pioter, closed her eyes, and with both her hands held his face and pulled his body towards her. Pioter laid her on the floor, and in a flash, he took her clothes from her. Valia's breasts amazed Pioter with their size and their beauty, and the two made love for an entire hour without stopping.

"Valia, Valia," a male voice called her from outside. Valia went out, exchanged a few words with her brother in a language he couldn't understand, and came back.

"Who was that?" asked Pioter.

"That was my brother. He asked me about you, if you are a fugitive prisoner," she replied.

"What?" Pioter nervously asked and immediately got out of bed.

"Don't worry, dear," Valia consoled as she stood in front of him, caressing his beard to try to calm him down. "We don't hand over anyone. We don't like communists, because they always come and take things that belong to us. We want to be free, just like you."

"I must get out of here," said Pioter as he looked around for his clothes. Valia felt she couldn't resist the sexy look of his broad shoulders, and with sexual movements, she pulled him towards her.

"Where are you headed now?" she asked with compassion, as both of them snuggled in bed again.

"I have to get to Moscow. My friends are suffering in prison, even though they are all innocent. I escaped in order to save them, and so I have to reach Comrade Stalin fast and tell him what's really happening."

Suddenly, the footsteps of several people were heard approaching, and Pioter became nervous again. "It's alright. That's my brother, who has come with several of the town's leaders for you," Valia calmed him.

"Come for me?" wondered Pioter, when four strong men entered the tent, shaking his hand and sitting down on the carpet.

"We want to help you," Valia's brother began. "Come and tell us what you would like to do next, and we'll see how we can help. Valia told us that you are an intelligent and well-educated man, and we are aware of the fact that many smart people like you are being victimized by stupid men. Please tell us what you would like us to do for you. How can we help you?"

"The truth is," Pioter replied, half-shocked and half-smiling, "I am very surprised, and I am happy to make your acquaintance. It has been a long while since I have met good people, but I am on my way to Moscow. I have to reach Comrade Stalin to save many prisoners, my friends, who were given severe punishments, even though they did no wrong. Now it has really become complicated. They want to kill them because they demanded soap and towels."

"Soap and towels?" the town leaders asked.

"Yes, yes. Soap and towels. When the general prosecutor came to the prison we told him that disease was spreading and people were dying from lack of hygiene, so he decided that it would be much easier to wipe everybody out and to burn all the camps to the ground."

"What did you say? The General Commander? You must be joking!" the town leader interrupted him.

"No," answered Pioter. "I am not joking."

"Listen, my son. It's not that I don't believe your words, but I doubt if the General Commander could decide something so serious," the town leader continued, patting his beard. He had everyone's full attention as he continued, "This is not his decision. He is only the executor. Be very careful. Don't go to anyone and don't even say you are alive. You can't save the prisoners, and it is clear that they will kill you without a trace. They are skilled soldiers. There are scientists and great intellectuals among them. You must understand that they are very dangerous.

"I suggest you change your name immediately. We will help you with a new ID card, and you should continue on your way to a place where no one knows you. Listen to me, because this is the only solution that will keep you alive."

2⃞.

Five whole years had passed since Olga disappeared from Carl's life. Nikko grew up with no trace of his mother, and only the neighbor next door, Margarita, who would often play with him, served as some kind of a mother figure in his life.

"Do you want me to make you something tasty?" Margarita asked as she slowly went closer to Carl in between her games with Nikko. "Or would you rather I play a little on the piano for you?"

"No, thank you," Carl answered, smiling at her. "This piano has been closed since..."

"I know you are sad that your wife disappeared, but life goes on, Carl," she tried to encourage him. "You can't allow yourself to continue living this way. You already have a big boy, and in a year or two he will start asking questions. He will go looking for his mother, and when he doesn't find her, his life will be miserable."

"I still think that my Olga will come back. She will be able to survive. You'll see. Very soon we will go back to living together like a proper family. But in any case, thank you, Margarita, for everything you are doing for Nikko. I can see he loves you very much."

"And I love you," Margarita answered, as she made advances towards Carl. "I am prepared to do anything to give you and Nikko joy and happiness. I want him to be raised as a happy boy, and for him to even call me Mommy." Carl stood there embarrassed by her candidness, and remained silent. Margarita went down on her knees, started caressing his body and slowly unzipped the zipper in his pants. Carl, who was excited by her gentle and tender touch, kissed her and led her to the bedroom.

"Ahhhh!" Margarita screamed when Carl penetrated her body with his member.

"What's wrong?" he asked. Is everything alright?"

"Yes, go on Carl. I want you!" she replied as they made love.

"You are very young, aren't you?" asked Carl.

"I am already 17 years old, and this is my first time," she said. "I never made love to a man before."

"Ah, really?" Carl said in a surprised voice. "And do you know that I am 17 years older than you?"

"I know Carl, and I really don't care how old you are," she kissed his lips. "I have been loving you and wanting only you for a long time. You are the youngest and best man for me!"

Compared to the revolution that was taking place in the prison camps, life in Helsinki seemed relaxed. "Comrade General Commander," a senior officer saluted his commander. "The tractors and the soldiers are prepared and ready for your orders!"

"Great. Now organize around the fence of Prison Number One. Tomorrow at 4 a.m. you should begin and within two hours I want to see you have finished and moved on to Prison Number Two and Prison Number Three. Is that understood?"

"Understood, commander!"

"Immediately after the operation, everyone must disappear!" the general shouted to the officers like a psychopath. "Everyone! Everyone must disappear!"

"And you," the commander said as turned to look at the wardens. "You will be able to head towards your homes and your families, so start mentally preparing. But now, leave me alone with the operation officer who was given orders to come. Go to sleep, and you will be updated in the morning." The guards left happy, and the General Commander stayed in front of the senior officers and the dozens of tractors and soldiers. "

"Are your orders clear?" he demanded to know. "Is everything clear?"

"Clear, Commander."

"Now, I want you to understand well the fine print in the operational orders," he continued. "Besides the fact that none of the prisoners here should remain living, none of them, after you are finished with them, you will move on to finish off the guards too. Is that clear? I have to have your full attention here, and you have to watch very well that not one of them escapes. This entire operation is top secret."

The noise of the tractor engines was heard at Felix's camp as well, and the fears and the speculations turned into a gloomy reality; everyone understood that the end was near. Prisoners began walking around the camp like ghosts, repenting. Why hadn't they listened to Felix, who warned them that the writing was on the wall. "Instead of sitting quietly, we should have attacked them already!" they were crying.

"What are YOU shouting about?" another prisoner shouted back. "You are the one who said that Felix was talking nonsense. They are coming to run us over! It's not enough that they caused millions of people to die here, they just don't care."

"When there was hunger in Russia, and Stalin was selling wheat abroad," Felix began, "he liked sending the message to the enemies in the west that we not only had food, but that we could even afford to sell it."

"He just wanted to see what dollars looked like," his friend smirked. "Today, we all understand that they are criminals. They are betraying the communist party, allegedly for the cause of social and political justice."

"Now it's a problem," continued Felix. "Now, we will not be able to break the fence. Look how many tractors and heroic soldiers have arrived."

"Some heroes," his friend interfered. "They kill innocent people, unarmed and innocent."

Felix put on a hat, opened both his arms and said a loud prayer:

"Hear O Israel, the Lord is our God, the Lord is One"

The prisoners, Jews and non-Jews alike, got chills. They all sympathized and put a hand over their eyes to recite the Shema prayer.

"This will save us, won't it?" whispered one of the Christian prisoners to Felix.

"Our God helps everyone. We don't have differences of nationality, religion, race or sex," he answered.

There was total darkness outside, and the smell of death was already in the air. The soldiers believed that all the prisoners in the camps had betrayed the Soviet people. They received an order to turn everyone to ashes and to bury them without mercy. They believed that the prisoners wanted to sell the Soviet Union to America, which had been known as a criminal country, with many junkies, negroes and inhumane citizens. Bombs fired from tanks were starting to reach Pioter's camp. The first group of prisoners fell, and they were killed one after the other. Soldiers were standing around the camp shooting without stopping, using guns identical to those of the Nazis.

"Let's go!" an officer ordered. "Get inside. No one can remain alive! No one!"

Pioter's friends decided that even if they had to die in this kind of war, without weapons, they would fight with their hands. Some of them confronted the soldiers, managed to take their weapons and returned fire.

"Stalin will save us!" was shouted by a number of prisoners. Suddenly from within the shooting, the conscience of several soldiers did not permit them to continue. Unable to bear the sight of dozens of unarmed men being run over and killed, they fled. Unlike them, the General Commander was smiling as he stood proudly on the hill, overlooking the operation. "The prisoners are stealing weapons from the soldiers, Comrade General," announced a general officer, who was standing by his side and looking for reasons to save his soldiers and leave. "You should also feel sorry for the soldiers," he said. "Look at how they are running away."

"They will be put to trial," responded the General Commander from Moscow as he kept smiling.

"My soldiers are still children. It's hard for them to kill in cold blood—you have to understand that," the officer said to persuade him.

"The only thing I understand, is that you are not on board with the general's decision!" the General Commander said as he glared at the officer. "An unwise decision! Not only your soldiers who are running away will be put to trial, but you will also have to prepare for such a trial, is that clear?"

"You are exaggerating a little, Comrade General Commander," the officer tried to appease him.

No more than thirty minutes later, the soldiers who tried to escape were caught and returned to the base. "I apologize," the general said before the General Commander had a chance to open his mouth. Even though he knew well what would be the results of his actions, he ignored them to apologize.

"Forgive me for sending you on such an unfair mission," he said as he shook their hands and quickly left.

"I have to speak to the defense ministry," he said to himself. "It's not possible that the army is degraded to such a level that they turn us into killers." As a first stage, he decided to summon all the officers for an urgent meeting.

"Dear friends," the general said to the officers. "In our operation in the prisoner camps, we are killing people without a trial, and I think that we are talking about innocent people. I know for certain that among the prisoners there are senior army officers, who refused to carry out similar orders. Scientists, writers, doctors. I checked the lists, and I didn't find even one killer there! Therefore, I summoned you now. I want to inform you that I, as a general in the army, am going to refuse an order, even though the meaning of refusing on the part of this country's leadership is clear to me." The general finished his words and went off the stage not expecting any response.

"There are senior officers in this room," a young officer added, identifying with the general's words. "We all fought the Nazis, and we saw what death was. We have also killed with our own hands, but we have never murdered captives." The officer stood proudly in the center of the room, "I am Major Tirkin, and I am prepared to refuse an order to kill innocent people." He went over to the general and saluted him with, "Comrade General, I join you, and I am prepared for any trial that will be required."

"Wait," another officer spoke up. "It's not so easy to resist. Three camps out of five have been completely annihilated. There is no trace of camps or prisoners remaining. But still …" he stopped and stood in front of the general as well. "I also agree with your words. This absurd theatre, these crimes against humanity—they will be remembered for generations, and as long as it is up to us, there will not be any more leaders who betray the people like this in order to remain in power. They are physically and morally killing us all. Therefore, I suggest we return to the ground immediately and save what is left!"

"Thank you very much!" said the general, who was moved by the officer's sympathy and started running with them towards the tanks and the tractors. The General Commander understood that the situation was becoming complicated and the officers were refusing to continue obeying his orders. He ran to the phone to report to the Kremlin, "Get me Lavrentiy Pavlovich Beria right away!" he shouted. "I'll show them what it means to refuse my orders," he started talking to himself. "It was all going so well until now. I have destroyed three camps, burying all the wise asses, and all of a sudden, this general comes along, this abominable criminal, and ruins my work. These prisoners may live and will tell the entire world the great crime that we..." he stopped, feeling that his thoughts were confusing, and he was referring to his own actions as "crimes. "It began with Stalin's order," he said to comfort himself, in case there would be questions.

"Hello, hello? Is this the Kremlin?" he asked when he heard a voice on the other side of the line. "It's the Soviet Union General Prosecutor talking. I need to speak urgently to Lavrentiy Pavlovich!"

"He is gone," the operator replied.

"So I wish to speak to Comrade Stalin then," he continued.

"Stalin is dead," she informed him.

"What? What?" he said as he became scared. "What did you say? It cannot be. When did this happen? Today? So let me talk to Khrushchev."

"They are all gone."

The General Prosecutor hung up the phone and made plans to leave the place as quickly as possible. He got into his military vehicle, and signaled the soldier to drive as fast as he could. The announcement about the death of the Leader of the Nations was starting to slowly reach all the officers, who treated it with restraint and fear.

Yusupov summoned the wardens of all the camps to his room. "Do you see the truck outside? It will take you all to the two nearby camps, and you will serve from there. Buy the prisoners soap and towels, and go now! That's an order!"

The wardens, who had dreamed of the upcoming vacation after the elimination of all the prisoners, were oblivious to the plan of their own destruction. They were surprised and remained silent upon receiving Yusupov's orders.

"Now, unfortunately, I have to inform you of the death of the Leader of the Nations, Comrade Stalin. I don't know how and what exactly happened, but he died today, and all the nations are grieving. As you can understand, this is a great loss to us all. Go in peace," he finished.

"And I thought that I was going to see my family soon," said one of the guards to his colleague on their way to the camps.

"It won't be so bad," his friend tried to console him. "All this has to end soon, and then you will see your family much faster than you think."

On their way to the camps, armed soldiers, who had not been informed of the changes, obeyed the order they received to eliminate the guards. They had been waiting for them by the lake, and within seconds after passing, they fired shots with submachines and killed them all.

20.

"Olga, Olga! You are not going to believe it!" Svetlana shouted as she ran towards Olga, who was busy breaking the ice to make room for the water. "Comrade Stalin is dead! He is deceased!"

"What?" Olga was surprised, and the hammer fell from her hands.

"It is safe to assume that there are going to be some changes now," commented Svetlana.

"I don't believe it's in our benefit," Olga answered. "But it's better this way. I hope that someday all these murderers will be judged. Yes, for taking Carl and my Nikko away from me too. He should be eight years old now. Can you believe it? My poor baby, I imagine that he is still looking for his mommy."

"Stop it, Olga. Don't get gloomy again. Let's continue working. By the end of the day, we have to get this entire mountain of ice broken down."

While everyone was whispering about Stalin's death, the camp continued to function as always. "Who is going to help us now?" a prisoner cried. "He was a good man, who took care of us so we didn't starve to death. He promised there would be free electricity, water and salt in every house. He wanted to build communism."

"What is that?" asked her cellmate.

"Well, it's when everyone eats the same thing and wears the same thing," she answered.

"So, who is going to help us now? Maybe America will help us, like it did during the war," she wondered.

"That's a big laugh. America was only standing in our way and preventing us from making a home. It's true that they sent us food during the war, but it was food that none of their citizens wanted to eat. Do you understand?" she asked. "They helped us in the war against Hitler, only to get part of Germany, Poland and Slovakia. What will happen to Russia now, I don't know. Who will help us live, like Stalin did?"

Lying in the upper bed in the cell, Olga listened to the conversation until she decided it was time to put in a word. "Honey," Olga called her. "Stalin would have only helped you die. I think the Americans are the ones who can help us, and this is the time that we need to find a way to let them know about what is going on here."

"Why do you think they will help you?" asked the prisoner. "Why do they care about us? Do you think they care about you?"

"I have read a lot about them," Olga explained. "I read that they were honest people, so much so that 86% percent of them have never lied in their lives! I want to believe now that the old man is dead, something can change for the better. The entire world is talking about him being a dictator, haven't you heard? He had no mercy on anyone. He even abandoned his own son. It's true that we all thought at first that he was for justice and peace, but it turns out that sometimes the lambs are smarter than the lions."

"He destroyed our country," Svetlana stepped in. "Go figure what will happen next. Maybe there will be civil strife now, with every one of the senior officers fighting for his position in leadership."

"Maybe now is our time, indeed," Olga thought out loud. "Maybe now we will not even be allowed to work here anymore. We need freedom, and then we will manage with all the rest."

"I heard that in the surviving men's camp, there is a 17-year-old guy from Leningrad named Felix, who has been writing letters to the Americans," another prisoner said. "He is in prison, because he wrote poems against Stalin and shared them. I heard he sent letters to the Americans and to the British too."

"That is a true hero," Svetlana said. "With such a guy, I would go to the end of the world."

"Good for him!" the girls agreed.

"There was another good guy there," the prisoner continued. "His name was Pioter, a biology professor. They forced him to conduct biological tests on people."

"What do you mean was?" asked Olga. "Was he in one of the camps that was destroyed?"

"I heard that he managed to get away before the destruction," another prisoner, who was a rat, commented.

"How did you hear that?" asked the girls curiously. "How did he succeed?"

"I know he tried to convince the prisoners to be one step ahead of the authorities, and before they came with tanks, to try to destroy them," she said.

"That's a good idea," said Olga.

"Yes, but not everyone agreed with him. There weren't many prisoners in that camp, and they didn't believe they would be able to pull it off."

"They may have been a minority," continued Olga, "but we are 4,000 prisoners in here! Let's take his idea and attack the guards. We will definitely manage to defeat them. What do you say? I want us to agree now, so there are no differences between us."

"Whoever doesn't want to run, raise her hand." Olga stood on the chair and called out, but no one raised her hand. "Now then. Who wants to?" All the girls raised their hands.

"I don't mind dying," shouted one of the prisoners, "but killing at least one of them is enough for me."

"They will not be able to destroy us!" Olga stood up and called out. "We have all fought against the fascists and spilled our blood and our family's blood for every square inch of this land! And what did our lovely leadership do? Stalin, Beria and this entire monstrous party sentenced us and put us in jail for decades, as if we were traitors."

"This is not a prison either," Svetlana interrupted. "This is one big grave, in which we are all going to die."

"Now is our time, girls!" Olga continued. "We have enough decent leaders in this country. It's time for us to get up and awaken them. But first, we have to choose a small committee of six or seven girls that will sit down and make an organized escape plan."

While the girls were sitting and planning an escape plan from the women's prison, in Felix's camp the prisoners were still stunned by the fact that almost 8,000 prisoners had been killed in three camps, and they were all allegedly accused of betraying the state.

"We have to attack!" Felix shouted. "I have combat experience against the enemy, and I am sure you will all demonstrate abilities as we go along."

"We don't really have any other choice," one of the prisoners agreed. "We have irons and chains we found in the icebergs, and even a few knives."

"It's set then," Felix happy concluded. "Let's select a committee of men with combat experience from among us and let's go!"

21.

It was 3 a.m. The guards shined the lamps around the camp and went to rest, while behind the fence over the mountain of icebergs, American soldiers were hiding, directing automatic weapons towards the camp. "It's time," one American officer smiled at his colleague. "Now we can attack the guards, but only with rubber bullets."

"Fire!" he gave the order and there was great noise heard from within the camp. Guards and prisoners seemed to be in a frenzy to save their lives. "Hands up!" was shouted towards the crowd in an indiscernible Russian. After less than thirty minutes, all the prisoners in the men's and women's camps had come to life.

"You are free!" called the American soldiers, who stood proud adorned with warm and beautiful attire with fur coats and hats, giving the prisoners warm clothes and all sorts of candies. "We will take you anywhere you choose," said the captain. "We will board the ship, and everyone will board at whichever shore they choose."

"Even America?" asked one of the prisoners with excitement. "Even America," responded the officer with a smile. The joy in the camps was immense. From the dozens of kilometers that separate them, male and female prisoners met and were seen singing, dancing, crying, hugging each other, and some were praying and thanking the Lord. "Thank God! Thank you America," yelled one of the prisoners. "I am not going back to the Soviet Union!" said another prisoner. "I will not take the risk of going back to a country of slaves."

"You are right! They eliminate people for their loyalty in the Soviet Union. Let's go to America!"

Lieutenant colonel Yusupov, who has been put at the top of the people that have been interrogated, notices Olga and Svetlana outside and starts trembling. "Crime does not pay!" yelled Olga. "You will get your punishment at the right place and at the right time," she looked at him angrily. "And don't you think that the Americans are going to be those who will put you to trial," Svetlana interfered. "WE will take care of you and your friends. Mark my words. I promise you."

"Excuse me, miss," An American officer turned to Olga, looking all dressed up and polished. "Do you speak English?"

"Yes, sir," Olga responded, and even though she was still wearing her prisoner's outfit, she looked beautiful. "And how long was the young and beautiful lady in prison?"

"It has been eight years, one month and a day since I was incarcerated."

"And if I may ask, are you married?"

"Oh... my husband and my son are somewhere in Helsinki. They are probably still looking for me..." said Olga, and couldn't control the tears that started pouring from her eyes.

"Calm down, madam. I think we can help you," the American commander smiled at her, and placed his hand gently on her shoulder.

"Dear friends!" a voice in the speaker system sounded in the Russian language, and interrupted the conversation between them. "You have two days to decide who is going with us, and who continues on his own. Now, everyone is invited to the dining room. Your lunch is ready." Loud applause of great joy sounded everywhere; it was a joy that they haven't felt in years and weren't expecting to come.

"Would you believe it?" Svetlana hugged Olga on the way to the dining room. "The truth is that you were the one who has strengthened me," Olga told her. "But with a way to go to the Americans, no doubt. Look how they care about other people. I wish all the nations would take care of each other like that, and no one suffers like we have suffered. Despotism is a crime against humanity. Now, someone has to assume real leadership and put an end to this dictatorship!"

"What are your plans, Olga? Should we go see what Yusupov's fate is?"

"I am not going anywhere, I have to get to Helsinki to my husband and to my dear son."

"Wait, Olga. We can't go until he is punished. Such a person cannot escape from what he has done to us. Don't forget that he wanted to rape us and kill us too. How can we let him get away?"

"What do you suggest? That we kill him ourselves, or that we take him to America?" Olga laughed. "Neither, we have to make sure he is punished, along with all those that sent him."

"You can take care of that from America, you know. We have to raise a universal cry, and we can't do that now and from here."

"The entire bureau of the communist party is a bunch of killers," Felix's voice sounded, joining the girls with his food tray. "Nice to meet you, I'm Felix."

"You're Felix?!"

"I have heard about you too. Olga and Svetlana, am I wrong?"

"No, no, come sit with us."

"I agree with you that we should raise a universal cry. Our friends here have paid with their lives only for asking some soap and towels. The entire free world has to fight these barbarians. If we don't try to fight now, later it will be too late. But we can't do it just now."

"You see?" Olga reproached Svetlana and turned to Felix: "Franco and Hitler proved it. They have annihilated six million Jews without thinking for a minute, just for refusing to give them money in their war against the Soviet Union. Hitler and his gang managed to sell the Germans a so-called social-democracy, as a way of saving them from the same dictatorship. They just forgot to mention that they were going to destroy entire nations, with no connection to communism."

"You are right," Felix referred to what she said. "I will try to turn to the authorities and we'll see what we can do." He finished eating, got up and hugged the girls. "I'll see you in our Motherland," he said turning to look at Olga: "Take care of yourself! I know it will be hard for you to go to Helsinki, but try to get aid from the Red Cross."

Svetlana started crying, partly from happiness, but also from sadness. "It's hard for me to part with you, Olga," she hugged her tightly. "I wanted to go everywhere with you, even now before we go back to our families, but I don't really believe it can be changed. Felix is right. Go on your way. You have to get back to your little Nikolai. Think about him, then about the state."

"I don't know about you," another prisoner joined the conversation, "but I don't know if I want return to Russia, after the accusations and the unjust punishment I received for no reason. I think I would rather live in a foreign country than to suffer for the rest of my days in my own Motherland."

"I think the same way," a different prisoner added, "and I know of more prisoners like us, that despite being released, don't really want to go back home. The choice has to be for a free country, where we can breathe fresh air, with no fear of jail."

While the discussion continued, most of the prisoners started walking away and disappearing into the mist. Slowly a complete silence was created, and the undecided found themselves sadly returning to their cells. "The chairman of the communist party, Nikita Khrushchev, has liberated you!" the new warden announced. "He has also erased all the indictments and charges of alleged treason. From now on, you are free from all sentences, and you can go back to a life of labor and the construction of the Motherland. Are there any questions?"

"Yes," a young man raised his hand. "Excuse me, but I'm not from Russia, and I would like to build my Motherland, which is Georgia. Can I? Am I also free to go to my home and to my family?"

"What were you sentenced for?" asked the warden.

"I am a school teacher, and I got 25 years in jail for saying that Stalin was a little tough. I'd like to go back to school," he replied.

"What is your name?" the warden questioned him.

"Gogia," he answered.

"You better not say anymore, Gogia," said the warden, and all the prisoners started laughing. "The Soviets' compassion is only on paper," he said as he turned to everybody. "You should always think well about every word you say. Otherwise, the snitches will have to report it, like before. Remember that it is forbidden to stand on the street and talk in groups of three people or more. In the eyes of the police, that is still considered a demonstration, and they will disperse you. If you don't part, they will send you to prison. And if you resist, the penalty can be very severe. Got it? Now go on your way."

Olga, who seemed to be stronger than ever, joined the thousands of prisoners that started walking. Some wounded, in torn clothes, leaning on sticks, barefoot. There was no trace of soldiers with guns and dogs, but in between muddy puddles and melting ice, some almost collapsed. "We have been through much worse things together," yelled Olga at everyone. "A little more and we'll be home!"

"God in heaven," cried an elderly man. "You have taken the Jews out of Egypt from slavery to freedom, please help us return home."

"Wait, I already see houses on the horizon," called one of the prisoners, and within seconds, dozens of men from the nearby village appeared in front of them.

"Let's go, friends. We will feed you right away," called the head of the village.

"Bring any food you can from your homes, especially fats. Give it to them, and then give them a warm place to sleep, but not for too long, for they can die in their sleep.

Therefore, after an hour or two, wake them up and let them drink again."

Olga was among the first people who reached the train station. "Give priority to women and elderly citizens," she cried out loud. "There are 14 cars here, but there won't be enough places for everyone, and you must be considerate of others."

"Who do you think you are?" scolded the station manager.

"I suggest you stay out of it. Just go with the flow," said one of the older prisoners as he boarded the train.

"I have to sit next to you," said a prisoner who entered the packed train to a man who was sitting squished into a corner. But she immediately turned her behind to him.

"It has been ten years since I have felt a woman," the man whispered to her. The woman turned her head towards him and started kissing him. The man took out his penis, and the two started making love on the train.

20.

Eight years, a month and a day, after being humiliated as a hopeless prisoner, Olga returned to the streets of Leningrad, her hometown, which seemed full of life. Shops, restaurants and people in beautiful clothes with smiling children were running around. Olga stood in the middle of the street barefoot, crying and remembering her mother, who risked her life in the war, and Carl her love.

"It's so good to be home," she said to herself, "where I grew up and used to be happy. I even brought Carl here, when I gave myself to him for the first time. Carl, my love. Oh, the passion that we used to have," she thought to herself, when suddenly the sound of a guitar playing Marc Brent's "The Beloved City," caught her attention. Olga stopped, sat on the street corner and started crying.

"What is that? Did they remodel the houses here?" She went up to her house, just like she used to do when she was a little girl, and ran up the stairs, expecting her mother to open the door and welcome her with a warm embrace. The keys to the house weren't on the doorpost, like she thought. "Maybe under the rug?" she said to herself. Feeling helpless, she sat on the ground and started crying again. The neighbor's door opened.

"Aunt Tanya?" Olga was surprised to see her neighbor, whom she used to call "aunt" when she was still a child.

"Who are you, madam?" the neighbor asked puzzled, when she heard Olga calling her name.

"Don't you remember me? I am Olga, Vera's daughter," she answered.

"Olechka," the neighbor said as she went closer to her and caressed her face. "It's impossible. What happened to you? Where are your clothes from? Where are your shoes? Aren't you in Helsinki with your son?"

"No, Aunt Tanya. I did go to Helsinki, but..."

"Come. Come inside, dear. You must rest," she hugged her lovingly.

"You know, many things have changed here," Tanya said, happy to finally have someone to talk to. Olga was making her loneliness disappear. "When you left for Helsinki, Leningrad received the Lenin Award, which you must know is considered to be the highest award in the Soviet Union."

"Yes, yes," Olga nodded and signaled Tanya with her head to continue.

"I thought about you and Vera, for who deserved the medal and the title "Soldiers with Extraordinary Courage" more than you?"

Olga restrained herself from showing her excitement, so that Tanya wouldn't stop telling the story. "Now, that Stalin is dead," continued the neighbor, "Khrushchev is in power, and he practically defames the worship of Stalin. I don't understand how we didn't see it happening. I was one of those people who admired Stalin at the time."

"Never mind, because since then they have begun to build new residential neighborhoods and government and public buildings. You can see that they have even renovated this building. In short, dear Olechka, from the bombed, starving, frozen and bleeding Leningrad that you remember, the city advanced. It is developing and turning into a city full of life."

"And what is happening with Mom's apartment now?" Olga asked. "Is anyone living there?"

"It's the new party chairman in the city. He is the one who is living in your apartment now. He is such a snob. He brags all day long about his chauffeur and his vehicle. You better not mess with him, he can only harm you."

"I have been through so much, Tanya, that I am no longer afraid of anyone. After eight years in prison, he can't take my home away from me," Olga got up and left Tanya's house. As she sat near the door to her house, she dozed off.

"Who is this prostitute?" the party leader asked and woke Olga from her sleep. "Get her out of here!" he ordered his bodyguard.

Olga didn't budge. "This is my house. Why should I go? And where exactly would I go? I have no other house, or any other country," she told him.

"You better go now, do you understand?"

Olga stood in front of him determined and said, "I am not moving from here!"

"I understand you want the militia to deal with you," the chairman said as he opened the apartment and went inside. Olga seized the moment, shoved the bodyguard aside and went in. "Get out, you insolent woman. You can't soil my apartment!" yelled the chairman.

"You are the insolent one! Look, these are even our table and chairs, and this is our closet too, and you are telling me I am insolent? You get out of here, right now. This is my house. You don't scare me with your militia," she told him.

"Who do you think you are?" the chairman asked, losing his patience.

"Listen well, mister!" Olga said as she stood in front of him. "I just came back from prison, after many years, do you understand? Your militia and the KGB sent me for 25 years for doing nothing wrong! So after years of suffering, when I get out, you steal my apartment? How dare you? And to sleep on my bed? To eat at my table? Who are you, as a member of the communist party, to behave that way and threaten me with the militia? It's time for you all to stop this horrific behavior against innocent citizens, who only oppose your corruption."

"I am here, and nothing is going to change that. You don't have many choices, missy, so pick yourself up and leave!" he ordered.

"Don't you fool yourself! I don't even want to live in this country, and it's not because I don't love it, but because people like you force me to run away," she began. "I even married a Finnish man. They refused to marry us here, even though he fought for Russia. Was that all just so you could walk around here with your bodyguard and your personal chauffeur?"

"OK," the chairman lowered his tone. "I won't call the militia, but I suggest you clear out of the apartment."

After pouring her heart out, Olga decided to go onto the streets of Leningrad to think of a plan for the rest of her travels. With supplies her Aunt Tanya had given her, she boarded a train, lay down on one of the seats and woke up all alone. Everything she had with her had been stolen. Olga, who had been through worse, didn't take it personally, but she made a decision. She would continue towards the offices of the city hall and request permission to leave the Soviet Union.

The clerks, who saw only a young woman with torn clothes and who was dirty from head to toe, did not take her seriously. "You have to submit a written request to the management and they will send you a reply," said a clerk in the population department, and then turned his back on her.

"But I don't have an address," Olga reminded the clerk. "And besides, there is someone else living in my house today."

"So where are you sleeping?" a female clerk, who pitied Olga, asked.

"Nowhere," Olga lowered her eyes. "How long will it take?"

"A month or two. You can write you're homeless," she suggested.

Olga left the office, lost and searching for her way. People saw her on the street and tried to help her, but she refused and with her remaining strength, she boarded a train.

"There is no room, lady. All the seats are taken," one of the passengers told her and tried to take her off the train.

Olga fainted and fell to the floor, until someone shouted, "Water! Someone bring some water!" as a crowd formed around her.

"What is happening there?" called out Carl, who was coincidentally passing by at that particular place at the same time.

"Nothing special," replied a passerby. "Some poor woman fell. She must be sick. We should order an ambulance for her." Carl left the scene, continuing to search for Olga on the city streets, and refusing to lose hope.

Felix left the ship, unable to believe that there were no guards around waiting to kill him, be it for ten days vacation, and perhaps a promotion. "I hope you are free, my son, and that you will not have to run away again," his father, a philosophy professor, who was an old member of the communist party, welcomed him. "It is different now, and we can live quietly," he added.

"What are you talking about, Dad?" Felix interrupted.

"Stalin is dead, and Khrushchev is starting to talk about his errors, about what a dictator he was and how the entire party leadership was afraid of him," explained his father.

"I can't sit still, Dad. Especially not now. Not after everything I saw in prison. I don't believe one word from them, and I cannot close my eyes and shut my ears. I beg you to forgive me, Father. I know you want to make order in Russia too, but they won't let you do a thing. You will be considered a traitor."

"Tell me, son," his father asked. "What exactly happened there and how were you released?"

"I kept repeating the "Shema Israel," so that God would keep me safe and would protect you. Thank God, nothing happened. But Dad, I wasn't released. I was saved thanks to the American soldiers, who came in battle ships and liberated us all. They are good people, and they even took whoever wanted, with them to America. Don't you understand that now Russia can no longer exist in hostility?

Russia needs to build friendships with other countries, but the communists are closing in on all of us. If we keep silent, we will always remain slaves. They kill anyone who moves— this is the criminal way, Dad. Why do you think they don't let us leave Russia easily? They are afraid that we will find out that life is better in other places."

"The important thing is that you are free now," his father said and hugged him. "But you have to understand, son, that you can't build a better life outside for yourself and even for all of humanity, if your family suffers here in Russia. You do know that this is what is going to happen, don't you?"

"I can no longer back out," he replied.

"So why didn't you go straight to Canada or America? You could have moved on to Israel from there, and built your own country, son. Why did you miss such an opportunity? You know that eventually we will all get to the land of our forefathers. That is the true motherland of us all. Today, I don't think that any of us will ever be able to convince the Russians to change their policies. Take Germany for example, where millions of Jews lived for thousands of years, until the minute the anti-Semite Hitler wanted them to give him money to go to war with Russia. Like any lazy person who wants money without work, he thought that others should support him. He was so angry that he decided to get even. You have to understand, my son, that we have no future anywhere else, other than our true country, which is Israel. I am telling you that honestly, and if I was any younger, I'd sacrifice myself for Israel."

"You are right, Dad. I think you are a real father and a good son of the people of Israel," Felix hugged him. "Let's go to sleep. I am tired."

Felix finally had a night of restful sleep. At dawn, he went for a walk on the streets of Noski Prospekt and sat at the Pushkin Cafe. Felix watched the passersby in front of him; men and women hurrying for work, children going to school and drunks sleeping in their feces. He tore the paper from his cigarettes, grabbed a pen and began to write again.

Young Sergei, who got something Felix wrote, went over to his father to show him. "Does that mean Felix is back?" he asked. The father was surprised.

"Who is Felix, Dad?" asked the lad.

"Felix was a famous anti-Stalin songwriter, and I haven't seen or heard anything from him for years, but now he is probably back and writing against the entire leadership. Don't read it, son, and don't take anything from him. If it becomes known you are reading his poems, you will have big problems!" the father advised.

"Those days are gone, Father," the son began. I heard about the time that Stalin used to arrest people to get free working hands for construction projects in Siberia, Kamchatka and Belomorkanal. But a short time afterwards, everyone died and their bodies were buried in unknown places. Now it's different, Father. Now, no one will allow anyone to act like Stalin."

Felix continued to write day and night, tirelessly, and more than ever before. In some of his poems he even called Khrushchev a pig that was born from a dog. He published his poems in popular places and threw them everywhere. There were even some who identified with his words to such an extent that they searched for his poems. After a short while, the rumor reached the KGB, and they put out an order to arrest him and to take care of him without delay. The order reached Felix, so he decided to change his approach. From the noisy streets in the afternoon, he moved on to deliver his poems via post office boxes late at night.

"Whoever catches Felix will get an award from Comrade Khrushchev," yelled the KGB commander to his officers.

"The truth is," one of the officers whispered to his colleague, "Khrushchev really does look like a pig."

"Ha, ha!" he laughed. "But an order is an order, bro."

Felix continued his work in Moscow, and the KGB members found him on his way to the train and whispered between themselves. They saw Felix buying a ticket, entering the train, taking a newspaper, sitting down and reading. Out of the corner of his eye, he noticed two detectives coming towards him. With swift movements, he pulled out a pack of cigarettes and pretended to go out to smoke. The train was going very fast, and Felix changed his direction. The detectives ran after him, pulled out their guns and were ready to kill him. Felix managed to find a dark corner, and stood behind the door. When the detectives came, Felix opened the door and hit one of the officers hard before running out. The second detective spared his colleague, who fainted and fell to the floor. Raising his head, he saw Felix and shot in all directions. Felix was injured in the leg. He tried to hold on to the handle of the car, but the officer continued shooting and Felix lost control and fell from the train into the deep abyss.

2⃞.

The rumors about the release of the prisoners reached Maximov's ears as well; he hurried to search for Olga. In his lieutenant colonel uniform, he proudly knocked on her door, expecting and hoping for good news. "I'm sorry if I am disturbing anyone," he told the party member's bodyguard, who opened the door. "I just wanted to know if there was a young girl who came here recently?"

In complete silence, the bodyguard looked back and stepped outside. "The truth is there was," he whispered to Maximov. "There was someone here yesterday. I wouldn't say she was so young, but she did say it was her house."

"And what happened? Where did she go?" Maximov's eyes opened wide.

"I have no idea. She went out into the street," the guard answered, and signaled Maximov that he could not elaborate on the subject any further.

"She is alive! She is alive!" Maximov said to himself and happily ran outside to try to locate Olga on the city streets.

"Search the streets, but mainly those in the center," he ordered his soldiers. "This lady is top priority."

The joy Maximov felt from knowing that Olga was alive was not shared by Carl, who was sitting in a cafe in the city. Exhausted and assuming there was no point in searching anymore, he took a newspaper in his hands and was surprised at the main headline:

"Khrushchev Releases Thousands of Political Prisoners"

I can't believe it," Carl trembled and called the waitress. "Look, look! My wife is free, look!" He stood up and started kissing her. "I have to find her. God please, let her be alive. I am begging," he called out and looked up at the sky. "I will go to her mother's house, maybe she is already there."

"I have nothing to tell you, boy. There is no girl here," the member of the party told him.

"Wait," Carl held the door, before it was slammed shut. "I am not saying she is here, but this is her house. Maybe if she didn't come until now, she will come later. All I am asking is that you tell her that her husband is looking for her." Before Carl was able to finish his words, the party member slammed the door in his face. Carl continued knocking. "I don't want anything from you, I swear. I just want to know that she is alive!" he shouted.

In a moment of compassion, the man opened the door and told him, "There was a woman here yesterday. She was dressed in a prisoner's uniform. Could it be that she is the one you are looking for?"

"Yes, yes, thank you! What did she say?" he questioned.

"She claimed this was her house, and she had been in prison for eight years. She went on to say that she had been exonerated."

"Wow. I don't believe it—my Olga is alive! Do you maybe know where she might have gone?"

"No, I don't. But there was a lieutenant colonel here this morning, who my bodyguard told me was also looking for her. Maybe he's her father, I don't know. Now, leave me alone." The door slammed, and the shocked Carl sat down on the floor, "Thank you, thank you, dear God! Thank you!"

Happy as could be, Carl hopped joyfully around the city, stopping to hug people, thinking to himself how Nikko's face will light up when he tells him his mother is alive. "My Olga is alive! My Olga is alive!"

"I am sorry to tell you, Olga, that I have to hospitalize you," the doctor told her. "You have tuberculosis, and it would be irresponsible on my part to let you go."

"No, doctor, I can't. There are people waiting for me in Helsinki," Olga became nervous. "My son Nikko and my husband, who haven't seen me for eight years!"

"Why?" asked the doctor.

"I was in prison, because I was sentenced for high treason. After Stalin died, Khrushchev exonerated me, and now I am waiting for a permit to allow me to go to my family."

"Oh my," the doctor said to himself. "This woman can really get me in trouble."

"I will sign your papers and tomorrow you will leave safely," he said as he left the room.

The hearing in city hall concerning Olga was underway, but there were differing opinions. "She knows too many things—things that we don't want her telling abroad," said the chairman of the committee who was in charge of authorizing trips. "I think that we already have a decision here. Does anyone have anything to add?"

"Yes," a member of the committee raised her hand. "I can see she has been exonerated from all charges against her, and besides, she is married and she has a child. He should be eleven now, and he is waiting for his mother. It would be immoral to separate the mother from her son and her husband."

"There are more details here," added another member while she was reading Olga's personal file. "It says here she fought the Gestapo, and even participated in the breaking of the siege on Leningrad. I, as a Soviet citizen, can't allow myself to keep her from going back to her family. We can't just throw her out onto the street."

"But what do you think is going to happen if she goes to the Finnish embassy and tells them everything?" asked the chairman of the committee.

"I have an idea," one of the members who identified with Olga jumped up. "I suggest we first give her a place to live here. Later we can turn to Moscow and try to get a permit for her to immigrate abroad. What do you say?"

There was silence in the room. Eleven members remained quiet. "We can't give an apartment to such a serious prisoner, and that is final!" said the chairman and closed the meeting.

Olga continued to go to city hall every day, expecting her salvation. Rejected over and over again, she was requested to leave the place. After a week, she decided that she wasn't going to leave city hall without an answer. "Out, out!" the clerk yelled at her.

"Today, I am not going anywhere until I get an answer." Olga sat down and wouldn't get up.

"Throw her outside," the clerk ordered the security guards, who held her arms and tried to evict her.

"I have spilled blood for you, and you don't deserve to represent us. I have nowhere to go, please," she shouted, which drew a crowd of curious people around her. Olga fought the security guards with all her strength.

"Take her to prison! She is used to that," the clerk yelled.

"Boo to the police," people in the crowd cried out.

Among the passersby that day was Maximov, who was still searching for Olga. He tried to pass to the other side of the street when he suddenly saw her in the hands of the cops. "Olga, Olga!" he yelled from the top of his voice and ran towards her. "Move it! I'm her father," he attacked the police and rescued her. Olga seemed in shock, not understanding what was going on with her. "Olga, dear, it's me, Maximov," he looked into her eyes. "Do you recognize me?" Olga's eyes were filled with tears, feeling unable to utter a word. "Where have you been for so long? I have been looking everywhere for you." Olga hugged Maximov, burst out crying and the crowd around her was applauding. After a few minutes, Olga fainted. Maximov picked her up and took her to his home.

"How much she has suffered," Maximov thought as he was sitting next to Olga. He tucked her into a warm and cozy bed and told his wife, Tatyana, what had happened. "We have to help her. She is a true heroine. She is Vera's daughter. Do you remember I told you, that long before I found you on the stairwell, she was the love of my life? We liberated the city together, breaking down the siege!"

"Sure. Her picture was hanging in your apartment, in her army uniform. I remember being amazed by her beauty," she answered.

Olga opened her eyes, saw Maximov and started crying again. "Calm down, dear," Tatyana caressed her. "You are in a safe place. Get up slowly and eat something. You have new clothes here. Get up, dear."

"I have to go to Carl and my Nikko," she began. "Please, help me leave Russia."

"Do you have a son?" asked Tatyana.

"Yes." Olga answered, and started crying again. "I have a son, who no longer remembers me. I was arrested at the market in Helsinki–kidnapped without a word. They probably didn't tell Carl anything either, so I don't think he knows anything about what happened to me."

"I have to let him know I am here. That I am alive. Why don't I write him a letter?" she suggested.

"Write a letter? That's not going to be easy," Tatyana explained to her. "The censors will immediately destroy it."

"She is right," Maximov interrupted. "They don't even look and check. For them, everything is hermetically closed, with no exceptions. But you can try."

Olga didn't give up the opportunity, even if she didn't stand a chance. She sent Carl a letter, but she got no reply. She went to the Red Cross to ask for assistance, but she didn't get a response from them either.

The days went by and Olga, who remained with Maximov and Tatyana, continued writing to Carl every week, but it had been 16 years since the day she disappeared. One day Olga received a letter from Carl's brother:

Dear Olga,

I hope you are feeling well. I wanted to tell you that during all the years you have been missing Carl has been looking everywhere for you. When he heard you were released and you didn't even send one letter, he gave up, and for his own personal reasons he decided to get married.

Your son, Nikolai, serves in our country's defense forces. He knows only one mother, and that is Carl's current wife.

Carl and I reached a conclusion that today Nikko no longer needs to know that you are his mother – for his sake and for his future. The important thing is that he is happy.

Olga, I am asking you to stop writing and looking for him.

Take care of yourself.

Olga read the letter with rapid heartbeats. She finished the bottom line, suffered an asthma attack, and fell down unconscious.

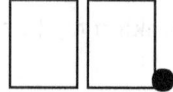

Maximov continued to activate his personal connections to get help rehabilitating Olga. He even managed to meet with a KGB general he knew from his position in the army. He got an apartment for her among scientists on the ground floor, and pension funds of about 35 rubles a month.

Olga's health was deteriorating, and she often had to be hospitalized or to call doctors for urgent help. "How is it possible that I am still alive, doctor?" Olga kept asking. "My son doesn't know, and will never know, who his mother is. Even if I die, he won't know who I am and what happened to me."

Olga decided to take a walk in all the places she had visited with Carl after the war. She passed the Laisakovsky resort garden, but instead of enjoying the spectacular landscape in front of her eyes, she became sad. Feeling faint, she sat down to rest on a bench near the Armenian church, where the drunk and the homeless would usually sleep.

A young couple, Rubbie and Fannie, who had known each other for only a few days, were enjoying their walk on the streets of Leningrad. They dined at the nearby Caucasus restaurant, where they were served authentic Georgian cuisine with luxury wines. "25 rubles," the waiter came said as he handed them the bill. Rubbie smiled, and left him thirty.

"That's a lot, isn't it?" Fannie asked. "You are aware that this is basically one-third of a doctor's monthly starting salary in the Soviet Union, don't you? My cousins, who have been senior engineers for many years, can't afford to spend these prices on a meal, not even once."

"Thank you very much," Rubbie said to the waiter and escorted Fannie outside, in the direction of the Armenian church.

"What a poor drunk," Fannie said, feeling the need to go help Olga, who had been lying on the bench, making strange noises.

"I don't think she is drunk," Rubbie added as he tried to come close and take a look at her face. "It seems to me that she is just ill. Look, there's no smell of alcohol." Rubbie got closer to Olga, checked her pulse and yelled to Fannie, "Run to the church and call for a doctor. Fast! Hurry Fannie!" At the sound of the screams and the panic, a crowd gathered. An ambulance arrived and Fannie and Rubbie accompanied Olga to the hospital.

"What is her name?" the doctor asked.

"That truth is, we don't know," Rubbie answered him. Out of the corner of his eye he saw Olga opening her eyes, trying to wake up and fainting again.

"We must hospitalize her. Thank you both for your kindness," the doctor finished the conversation and turned to Olga to deliver first aid.

Rubbie went to his uncle's house and told his aunt and uncle how he started the day with great love and ended it with sadness and compassion.

"And who was she?" asked his Uncle Morris.

"I have no idea, Uncle, but I felt so sorry for her. It wasn't just that she looked ill, but she was also so lonely. I have no doubt there is a long life story behind her," he concluded.

"You did a good thing, dear. I am proud of you!" his uncle hugged him. "Tomorrow we will go to the hospital together and make sure that she is feeling better."

"Olga, this young man and his partner are the ones who saved you and brought you here. Without them, I doubt if you would have made it," the doctor told Olga.

"Hello, Olga," Rubbie presented himself gently. "And this is my uncle," he pointed to Morris, and Olga smiled.

"I work on a ship," he continued. "I wanted to let you know that if you need anything, just tell me."

"You should be proud of your nephew," Olga looked at Morris. "Tell me, did this charming lad serve in the war like you?" Olga tried to start a conversation.

"Sure. I served for six whole years. We fought in Japan and in Bandara. Why are you asking?" he enquired.

"I served too," Olga replied. "I fought to break the siege. The Gestapo captured of me, and my mother was killed. I escaped from prison, but after all that, I still can't believe I stayed alive."

"Do you have family?" Rubbie asked with interest.

"I have a son who should be your age now, but he doesn't know me. He and my husband are in Finland. I have been trying to get to them for years, but I couldn't," she began her sad tale.

Morris, who was fascinated with every word that came out of Olga's mouth, realized that the story was familiar to him. "Wait" he began. "Are you connected to Lieutenant Colonel Maximov?"

"Yes," Olga replied and stood up.

"That's it, I knew it!" he continued. "I have heard your story. I am so sad for you, but I think that one should never lose hope."

"Dear Olga," the doctor interrupted the conversation. "Your tests turned out well and you can go home."

"You see?" Morris rejoiced. "One should never lose hope!"

"We're in 1963, and it has already been 18 years since the KGB kidnapped me!" shouted Olga when she felt strong enough to go to the Finnish consulate again. "Do you understand that my son doesn't know me? 18 years! Have you any idea what it's like?"

"Come, sit down. Let's see what we can do," the ambassador invited her.

"I know that no one wants to fight with the authorities and the KGB on my account, but you have to understand that I am going to die, and this is my last chance to ask for help. The entire world is afraid of the Soviets. Everyone is supposedly acting nice, as if defending human rights, but it's just a game. Bottom line, they are doing nothing," she stated.

"What about the Red Cross, did you go to them?" the ambassador asked.

"Even the Red Cross can't help me. They censored all the letters I wrote to my husband," she told them. "The only thing that they did for me was to deliver a letter my husband's brother wrote to me."

"Well, that's good. So at least he knows that you are looking for him, doesn't he?" he asked.

"Well, no. In the letter, he informed me that my husband has started a new family, and that my son recognizes a stranger as his mother," she told him.

"I will check what I can do for you," the ambassador comforted her. "Now, go on your way, and we'll be in touch."

Close to her home, Olga was surprised to see Rubbie, who had been waiting for her with a pot of food his Uncle Morris sent her. "Rubbie dear, it's so good to see you," Olga greeted him. "Would you like to come up to my house?"

"I want you to tell me about your activity in the war," Rubbie said, trying to start a conversation with her.

"I'd be happy to," she smiled. "The truth is that you need to know the things I am about to tell you. You are part of the younger generation, who doesn't really know who the communists are. Would you believe me if I told you that they pretend to be peace seekers?"

"What do you mean?" asked Rubbie curiously.

"They pretend to get public support, but really they are killing many innocent people, only so they can be in power," she began. "They are corrupt and cruel. If no one rises against them, they will destroy the entire world."

"Are you talking about Russia?" he asked.

"Not just Russia. You can observe the communist method everywhere in the world; Africa, Asia and even in the Middle East. They all learned to solve things with force and violence. Read a little about China or Korea, and you will see that they are acting according to the methods of Stalin, Franco, Hitler and Mussolini. They are stripping the public of any free will. It cannot continue, it just can't!"

"What can we do, Olga? Who am I to be able to change anything?" Rubbie asked.

"You represent the future generation, and you can rise up with an agenda that will change the world. Build one big community, where everyone lives in peace and security, with no differences regarding nationality, skin color or world view. And then no nuclear weapons, bombers or tanks will be necessary. That way, people will invest in promoting industrial technology, and will probably also promote their level of living. I will die soon, but it's important for me that you will be able to change your future and that of young people like you. Hand-in-hand and without violence. Gather the majority who thinks the same, and you can change the world. Do you understand? Maybe someone like you can prevent a nuclear catastrophe, and give millions of people the right to live as they deserve."

"Olga, Olga," Rubbie called, seeing that Olga was becoming weak and her eyes were beginning to close.

"You know what I am dreaming about?" Olga woke up and continued speaking in a weak voice.

"Slowly, Olga. Don't stress," he told her. "What are you dreaming about?"

"About tomatoes and oranges. I guess people who eat a lot of them live longer," she smiled. "What do you live from?"

"I get a little pension, and that's enough for me to buy bread, salt, sugar, and a few potatoes. I am not the only one—there are many people who live like me. The important thing is that you are healthy, Olga. That is the most important thing."

"The only thing I still live for is the hope of seeing my Nikko," she continued." "I am sure he is handsome. He must be tall like his father and me. I pray to see him, at least one more time, even in a photo. After that, I don't mind dying."

"Don't talk nonsense. You are not going to die so fast," Rubbie tried to comfort her.

"If you had known me in Helsinki, you would have wanted to be my son too," she smiled. "I used to cook them soup like the one your aunt brought, and there was always joy in the house."

"I am happy you like the soup, Olga. With your permission, I must go now, but I will come to visit again."

For seven years, Rubbie continued visiting Olga, until Dr. Shapiro's fatal phone call, which led Rubbie to hurry and board the train. He reached 36/44 Dibonowski Street, where they had been treating Olga for more than eight hours. "Olga asks that you come in," Dr. Shapiro said to him. Rubbie, who had been sure he would never see Olga again, went to her room and hugged her.

"I have listened to you all these years, Olga dear. And now you have to listen to me," Rubbie started telling her. "There is no doubt that you are a hero! You are someone I will never forget and I will always try to be as much like you as I can. I want to tell you that just like when you were arrested in 1937, they also arrested my father, and I haven't seen him since. And that is not all. In 1946, they also arrested my brother, because they were afraid he would continue in my father's way, and my sister's husband too. Olga, you have to understand, my sister died at the age of 21 from a heart attack!"

Olga was stunned, and Rubbie, with tears in his eyes, continued pouring his heart to her. "Now, what I wanted to tell you was that they are teaching about acts of terrorism at the University of Patrice Lumumba in Moscow, and they are spreading flyers all over the world to organize provocations and Bolshevik revolutions. They are using innocent patriotic people to shake our stability. There is no one in the world who knows your suffering and that of my family. They all believe the lies that they tell them."

"The truth is, I am not surprised," Olga interrupted him.

"That's why," Rubbie continued, looking her straight in the eye, "you are like a mother to me, and I want to tell you that my mother and I have to leave the Soviet Union and to emigrate to Israel."

"What? Really?" Olga was surprised, trying to keep her eyes open, but feeling weaker than ever.

"I promise you, Olga Philipova, that I will look for your son, Nikolai, for as long as I live, and I will tell him everything. Everything."

"Thank you, Rubbie, but there is no need for you to bother so much on my account. All I ask is that you pray to your God to help me reach my son. I am sure that your God will understand me and take pity on me," she begged.

"I will pray, Olga, but you know that many Jewish families, who were mercilessly murdered, don't understand why God didn't have pity on the six million. I don't want you to get your hopes up, you know."

"I haven't cried for so many years," Olga said, unable to stop her tears. "There were always tears in my eyes, but I could never really cry."

"Cry, my Olga. Cry," Rubbie hugged her, unable to hide his tears and the sorrow he felt for her. "Go, go to your country, only leave me a photo, so I can look at you when I feel sad."

"I love you, Olga, and I will never forget you for as long as I live. You are a hero!" he assured her as he ran out the door.

31.

"What do you think about going to visit Leningrad?" Rubbie turned to his wife, Fannie, one quiet evening in the clear Jerusalem air. He was already 72 years old, the father of two and a grandfather of six. He had served in the Israel Defense Forces and participated in political committees for the renovation of the diplomatic relations with the Soviet Union.

"You know it's not called Leningrad anymore. They changed the name to Saint Petersburg, according to the political symbolism, for this is the pride of the Tsarist Empire. And indeed, since the name has been changed, the long awaited transformation has finally arrived, with all the changes that have taken place in the social and political life," Fannie answered him. "But I would love to go with you. I wonder what happened to your friend, Olga."

Only two weeks after making their decision, Rubbie and his wife arrived in their hometown, took the tram, and were surprised to find that just like when they were young, there was a small note on the window, saying "Number Two."

"Hello," Rubbie and Fannie called out as they entered Olga's little apartment, which on the outside looked just like it did forty years before. When they met an elderly woman, Rubbie asked, "Are you Olga Philipova?"

"No, Olga passed away a long time ago—in 1970, if I'm not mistaken."

"Oh," he became sad and turned to go.

Wait, wait a minute," the old lady stopped him. "This week I found this envelope here, that Miss Olga left before dying. I wanted to throw it away, but now, wait a minute."

After a few seconds, she returned and handed Rubbie the envelope. "Here, maybe it's for you."

"To my son Rubbie, from Olga."

Rubbie read what was written on the envelope and his eyes were filled with tears.

"I knew you would come back to Russia and that you wouldn't forget me. At least not you. Did you find Nikolai? Anyway, if you'd like to visit, I'd be happy if you can find my place of burial."

With great excitement, mixed with pain and compassion, Rubbie and Fannie continued to Helsinki. They went to the ministry for interior affairs, checked with personal connections and asked passersby, but all their attempts to try to locate some piece of information about Carl or Nikolai failed. "I guess the authorities destroyed all the sins and the inhumane deeds that they did," Rubbie decided. "Come Fanny, let's go home. If anyone wants to update us with any information they may find, they now have our address in Israel."

Two years had gone by when Rubbie received a telegram telling him about a man named Nikolai. He speaks Russian and it seemed like the person he was looking for had been found. Rubbie hurried to Helsinki, where he met the man and his friends at a fancy restaurant. "I don't really remember my mother," Nikolai started the conversation.

"Where did she come from?" Rubbie was interested.

"From Poland. I can tell you, from the photos I know she was a beautiful girl, a brunette. My parents got divorced when I was very young, so I can't really tell you anything about her."

Rubbie immediately understood that this was not the Nikolai he was looking for. Olga was a blond, and she definitely didn't divorce Carl. Rubbie thanked the people around him and bid them farewell.

Very disappointed, Rubbie returned to the airport. He stopped at the duty-free to buy himself coffee, just before boarding the flight. "Excuse me sir, what time is it?" he asked the first person he saw.

"Dvanachit," the guy mumbled in Russian. Rubbie looked in his eyes, as if he was certain he knew him from before.

"Is it possible that we know each other from some place?" Rubbie asked.

"I don't think so," replied the guy. "But nice to meet you." He extended his hand, saying, "I am Nikolai."

Rubbie was surprised at the sound of the name, and for a few seconds thoughts were running through his mind and he couldn't let go of the guy's hand. "Are you from Russia?" Rubbie tried to hide his embarrassment.

"No, the truth is I was never in Russia. My father was in the war, and he taught me some Russian. He fought against the Germans, and that is why he wanted me to learn Russian," he answered.

"Is your father alive?" Rubbie asked.

"Unfortunately, no. He passed away several years ago.

But he did tell me I was actually half-Russian," Nikolai answered, looking at his watch.

"Was your father's name Carl, by any chance?" Rubbie dared to ask, seeing Nikolai's paling face in front of him.

After a few long seconds, Nikolai lifted his head, put his suitcase on the floor and looked straight at Rubbie. "Who are you? How do you know my father's name?"

"What do you do today with your life?" Rubbie asked to try to make some more time.

"I am the Finnish deputy foreign minister, but what does that have to do with anything now. Who are you?" he asked again.

"Did your father participate in the war for breaking the siege?" he asked.

"Yes, how do you know that?" he demanded to know.

"Were you born in 1945?" he continued questioning.

"Yes. Yes. Yes. But would you stop asking me questions, and instead, just tell me who you are?"

"Let's sit for a few minutes," Rubbie suggested, placing a hand on his shoulder. "I am Rubbie from Israel. I am a writer, and the truth is I have been looking for you for a long time. I wrote a book about your mother, Olga, and about everything she had been through in the war and after it."

"But Olga is not my mother's name," Nikolai replied, unsure if he was mistaken.

"Olga is your real mother. She risked her life for you, and as far as I know, in the end she died from the sorrow of not being able to find you," he gently informed him.

Nikolai's eyes filled with tears. Rubbie stood up and hugged him, and Nikolai started crying like a little boy who had found his mother. "I knew it. I knew it when dad told me about the woman he loved so much in the war. He never mentioned her name, but I knew he was hiding something from me. I knew it!" he exclaimed.

Rubbie went to get something to drink, allowing Nikolai to calm down a bit and accept the news. With racing a heart and tearing eyes, Nikolai cancelled his business flight to Saint Petersburg and excused himself to go call his wife.

"Olga, honey. Tell Mom that I have an important thing to take care of, and that I will only arrive tomorrow. I don't have time to explain right now, but I will call you again later," he said and hung up the phone.

Rubbie's eyes opened wide, wondering if that was the hand of fate, or the power of the subconscious mind. "Regardless," Nikolai answered Rubbie's thoughts, which had been uttered without words, "I always thought that Olga was a very beautiful name, and that was what I named my eldest daughter."

And there it is. After a lifelong journey, without mother Olga, Nikolai went to her grave, unusually moved to see the writing on the tombstone:

"In my life and in my death, I will never forget my dear husband, Carl, and my beloved son, Nikolai, whom I didn't get to raise or see, but there wasn't a day that I did not think of him.

Farewell, my beloved."

www.ingramcontent.com/pod-product-compliance
Lightning Source LLC
Chambersburg PA
CBHW070109260626

47160CB00004B/1382